PRAISE F

* "[A] spectacularly realistic port. ___
former friends and the new girl in school . . ."
—*School Library Journal*, starred review, audio edition

"Strong voice and complex characters . . ." —*Booklist*

"The author's thoughtful and nonjudgmental approach creates an engaging, authentic portrayal of female friendship."
—*The Horn Book Guide*

"In her debut, Guerra demonstrates insight into the temptations and troubles of late adolescence, all rendered with nicely flowing prose and dialogue. She grounds her story in reality, and her characters come across as interesting, believable individuals, with Stella especially sympathetic and Ruby a standout original. . . . A strong new voice." —*Kirkus Reviews*

PRAISE FOR *BILLY THE KID IS NOT CRAZY:*

"Most readers, children and adults, will cheer for Billy instead of his folks the whole way through, even as he's acting up. . . . It's really hard not to like Billy." —*Kirkus Reviews*

BETTING BLIND

ALSO BY STEPHANIE GUERRA:

The Betting Blind Series:
Book One: *Betting Blind* (2014)
Book Two: *Out of Aces* (2015)

Torn
Billy the Kid Is Not Crazy

BETTING BLIND

STEPHANIE GUERRA

SKYSCAPE

Text copyright © 2014 Stephanie Guerra
All rights reserved.

Published by Skyscape, New York

www.apub.com

Amazon, the Amazon logo, and Skyscape are trademarks of Amazon.com, Inc., or its affiliates.

ISBN-13: 9781477847855
ISBN-10: 1477847855

Library of Congress Control Number: 2014935190

Printed in the United States of America

For my husband, Eric

*Many thanks to the Seattle Office of Arts & Culture
for its generous support.*

CHAPTER ONE

The first thing I did every morning was listen for Phil. He only came about once a week and never on the weekends. If he was there, I'd try to mess up his day a little before I left for school.

I sat up and kicked off my blanket. No voices . . . no laughter . . . but in the background, I could hear the soft thump of drums. Bad sign.

I rolled out of bed, brushed my teeth, and chugged the last inch of a day-old Red Bull. Then I pulled on jeans and a hoodie and headed downstairs. A pair of men's Italian brown leather shoes was sitting on the landing. I stepped on one, tried to scuff it.

"An absolute debacle, a political train wreck," Phil was saying over some cheesy jazz. The air smelled like breakfast. I turned into the living room.

"Hi, Gabe," Mom said. She and Phil were kicking it on the couch, Phil with a big plate of eggs on his belly and his arm slung around Mom's shoulder. Mom was in little pink pajamas that nobody over twenty should be rocking. She'd always been more of a hippie, but Phil had changed that—now she had the makeup, the nails, the dyed hair.

Phil was dressed for work. His shirt was unbuttoned at the top, and his nasty ape-chest was showing. Dude was nothing but a big roll of bills stuffed in a suit. He didn't even take off his wedding ring when he came to my place.

His face stretched in a fake smile. "Well, it's the young Brando." He adjusted his corporate toolbox glasses. "Good morning, Gabriel."

I didn't answer, just sat in the recliner across from them and kicked up my feet.

Mom gave me a look—*Please get out of here now*—but I pretended not to see.

"Well, it's what? Week two? How do you like your new school?" asked Phil.

"It's okay."

"Making any friends?"

"Not really. They're a bunch of future bankers who'll cheat on their wives in about twenty years." I stared at him. "What business trip are you on this time?"

Phil flushed, and Mom seriously turned maroon. "Gabriel! Into your room, now!"

"But I have school," I said. We both knew I didn't have to leave for another forty minutes.

"Go!" Mom said in a choked voice.

I got up, taking my time, grabbed a banana out of the fruit bowl in the kitchen, and went upstairs. I had a feeling Phil wouldn't stay much longer. I was right: a couple minutes later, the door slammed. I lay on my bed and ate the banana, wondering what it would take to make him leave forever.

Mom came up to my room. Her eyes were red, which made me feel like crap, because I didn't want to make her cry—just poke at him a little. She sat on the end of my bed. "Why can't you be decent to him?"

I sighed. "Because he's a jerk who's never going to leave his wife."

Mom glared at me and took a shaky breath, but she didn't answer. She knew I was right; she just didn't want to admit it, especially now that she had us trapped. We were doing okay before, living in White Center: she had a job at a café, and yeah, we lived in a crappy apartment, but so did everybody else. Now Phil was giving us free rent and he owned us.

I looked at Mom in those pink pajamas and said, "You could probably get your old job back. Or you could work for Frank at the insurance company." I tried to keep my voice calm. Mom had a hard time not getting emotional.

She shook her head and sure enough, tears started leaking out of her eyes. "You know I can't sit behind a desk all day! Why can't you just be happy? You can put Claremont High on your college applications! That's why we *moved* here!"

"No, you moved here for Phil."

"I moved here for your school! If you'd just try—"

I cut her off. "Don't go there." She was about to give me a speech I'd heard a million times, not that it ever did any good.

Mom stopped for a second. It was our dirty little secret that neither of us could deal with school. She'd dropped out her junior year, but she wanted so badly for things to be different for me. "I *am* going there. Maybe—"

"It doesn't matter where I go to school. It's not going to change anything!"

Mom wiped her eyes with the back of her hand. "Well, I don't agree with you. And you need to stop treating Phil this way. He owns this house."

My stomach twisted. I looked around my room: four white walls, a particleboard desk, and a bed. I hadn't even put up posters—that was how much I hated living on Phil's turf.

"Can you at least *try* to be nicer to him?"

"No."

"Please, Gabe. Where's the gentleman I raised?"

This was such a crazy question, I didn't even know how to answer. Mom was fuzzy-brained about a lot of things, including this whole idea of a *gentleman*. How could she talk about gentlemen when she was hooked up with a guy like Phil? And what was a gentleman, anyway? The only part of it I understood was that I was supposed to pay on dates and open doors for women (except the ones who didn't like it).

"Okay," I said to make her stop crying. Then, because I couldn't stand being home one second longer, I got up, bolted downstairs, and left for school. Even though it meant getting there early.

Claremont High was a training camp for rich people. It was a shock the first time I saw it. The floors were always clean, and there were twisted metal statues in the stairwells and big windows showing buzz-cut grass outside. The ceilings went up forever with cool beams and pipes at the top. Every classroom was tricked out with ceiling speakers, Smart Boards, and MacBooks—but most kids brought their own laptops or pads.

Now, two weeks in, it was starting to feel normal. I got to school early and sat in the quad, watching people drift in. A lot of the kids were what you'd expect from Microsoft Land, pulses ticking like bombs under their Abercrombie, all *I'm gonna beat you to Stanford and Silicon Valley and Googleplex!* But there were plenty of others, too, a bigger range than I'd expected.

When the bell finally rang, I headed to first-period science with Mr. Newport. He was a big guy with messy, curly hair. His pants were always droopy, his tie always loose, and his shirts looked like he'd ironed creases in them. I liked him for that.

As soon as the flood of people stopped, Newport held up a hand. "Don't put down your backpacks. We have to turn right around. The Microsoft Orchestra back-to-school concert is today."

Microsoft *Orchestra*?

I ended up in line next to Kyle Butler and Forrest Lexington, who ruled the school, along with their boy, Matt Chen. Kyle was a typical high school king. Dude had that surfer blond hair that girls love and a confident vibe like he knew how to have a good time; plus, he drove a Jag and dated Erin Fulman, the hottest girl in school. I think he was a rower. Forrest was harder to peg, but he was wicked smart and could talk circles around the teachers. I kind of liked him, for no good reason.

We headed downstairs to the auditorium and sat in the stadium seating, big fat plushed-out chairs like at the Cineplex. Kyle and Forrest broke out their phones and started texting. On my other side was an Asian guy plugged into a Kindle.

I wondered what my boys back at Jefferson were doing. Probably lighting blunts in the bathroom or texting through Hazlegrove's class. Maybe still at home sleeping. I wanted to make some guy friends at Claremont, but that takes time. Meanwhile, some girls—Jamie Elliott and her crew—were taking care of me, which was cool. Nothing like being adopted by a bunch of hotties.

"Oh damn, here it comes," Kyle said to Forrest. "Wait for it."

I glanced over, and they were both staring at the stage curtain, which was starting to open.

"She grew up, Daddy," breathed Forrest. "She ain't a little girl no more."

I looked at the musicians, dressed in black pants and white shirts, most of them about a hundred years old—and I saw who Forrest and Kyle were checking out.

There was a girl in front with a violin. She looked foreign, like Swedish or something. Her hair was blond, and she had slanted dark eyes and lips I could have sucked on for days. She was holding her violin under her chin, and she must have felt us staring, because she looked into the fourth row, right at us—and smiled.

"See that?" Kyle whispered. "She wants me!"

Forrest saw me looking and grinned. "That's Irina Petrova, dude," he told me. "It's okay. Go ahead and stare. We all do."

Kyle looked over, registering me for the first time.

"She's hot," I said. "How old is she?"

"Our age," said Kyle. "She used to go to school with us, but she's a music genius or something. Her parents pulled her out to homeschool."

"That was a sad day," said Forrest.

"Yeah, but it's not like she talked to anybody. She's . . ." Kyle made a stuck-up face.

"I'm going to get her number." *Why did I do that?*

Kyle said to Forrest, "Oh no, he didn't really just say that."

Forrest was nodding. "Yeah, he did. What's your name, dude?"

"Gabe." Well, I'd have to do it now.

"Good luck with that, Gabe," said Forrest.

"She's going to school you," said Kyle. "But credit for trying. If you even talk to her." He said it in a friendly way, and I could tell he thought I was all right. I smiled. It was actually the first nonschool conversation I'd had with guys since I started Claremont.

Principal Morrow tapped the mic. "Seniors, please join me in welcoming the Microsoft Orchestra." He clapped. After a second, so did everybody else.

Then the conductor lifted his stick, and the music started. The girl was a witch on her violin: all you could see was this sheet of blond hair and her bow ripping like a knife. After the first few songs, the other people stopped playing, and it was just her and this old man blazing out music. Even I could tell it was good.

I checked my phone. Twenty minutes left in first period. *Screw it.* I *was* going to get her number.

I got up and told Mr. Newport I had to go to the bathroom. Then I tried the doors in the hall until I found the one that led backstage. I opened it quietly and stuck my head in. Empty. I slid inside.

Backstage was dark and loud and messy, and it smelled like a basement. The musicians had left their cases and jackets lying everywhere. I couldn't help noticing that one of the jackets, tossed over a chair, had a big lump in the pocket. This was the kind of crowd that would carry cash and cards, maybe even checks . . . but I decided to leave it alone. I wasn't trying to get kicked out for theft.

I heard the applause, on and on. Finally the curtain opened, and people started coming through. A couple of them gave me weird looks, but mostly they ignored me. Then the girl walked past and crouched by a long black box.

She was ten times better up close. No detail left out, just damn perfect, even down to some freckles to make her look real. I walked over and said, "You were great."

She looked me up and down. "Thanks." She closed her violin box.

I was used to getting better reactions from girls, at least a smile. "What's your name?" I asked.

"Irina." Then she got up and started walking away. *Burn!*

I almost let her go, but I couldn't face those guys if I didn't get her number. Time to up my game. I followed her and said, "What was that song where it was just you and that old guy playing?"

"Mozart's Symphony number forty in G Minor," she said, still walking.

My neck was getting hot, but I made myself act completely calm, like when I'm bluffing through a bad hand in poker. "Do you know who does a good recording of that one?"

She turned and squinted at me. "Shouldn't you be in class?"

"Probably," I admitted. "Aren't you going to tell me, though?"

"My favorite is Karl Böhm and the Berlin Philharmonic." She gave me a little wave and walked fast down the stairs, kind of an obvious, *Don't follow me.*

But I had to. My manhood was at stake. I could see a straight ask was out of the question; no way would she give up the digits. So I said, "Hey, I know this is kind of weird, but I never heard anybody play the violin like that. Could I come watch the next time you play?"

She stopped walking and smiled—and I knew I was in. "Are you serious?" she said.

I nodded. "Yeah, you're really good."

"Well, we're performing at Seattle Center on Wednesday. But that's kind of soon."

"No, it's not. Can I text you or friend you or something, so I can get times and stuff?" I was already pulling my phone out of my pocket.

It took her a second, but she said, "Okay."

I handed it to her, and she punched in her digits and gave it back. It was harder than I usually had to work for a number, which made my phone feel like pure gold.

She walked away, didn't even say good-bye. I stood there for a second, grinning. Then I darted back into the auditorium just in time to grab my backpack before our row emptied. As I squeezed past Kyle and Forrest, I held out my phone.

"No," said Kyle. "You're lying."

"He's totally lying," said Forrest.

I showed them her number.

"You put that in yourself." But Kyle sounded amazed.

"Think whatever you want," I said. "It's the real thing." As we pushed out of the auditorium and into the hall, Kyle and Forrest kept staring at me.

"Is that really Irina Petrova's number?" Forrest demanded. "If you're screwing with us . . ."

"I'm not."

Forrest made little bowing motions. "You. Are my hero."

Kyle said, "You cracked the Rosetta stone, dude."

"I'm seeing her on Wednesday," I told them.

"Bastard!" said Kyle.

Forrest just shook his head. "Gotta hit calculus."

"You'll have to tell us about it. Take pictures," Kyle called as they went down the hall.

I couldn't stop smiling as I headed to the north wing for Algebra II.

Mr. Chatterjee had the softest, calmest voice, like something you'd listen to on purpose to go to sleep (as if math weren't enough). I sat in the back and searched Irina Petrova on my phone under the desk. She had about a hundred YouTube links. I clicked one, and at first I thought I'd gotten it wrong. The kid on there was six or seven, playing the violin on a big stage. But she had that same blond hair, and yeah, I decided it could be a younger Irina. I tried another, got the same thing—and then another tagged *Child Prodigy Plays Sonata in F Major*.

Irina was seriously a child prodigy? I always thought of them as nerds, not hot blondes. I guess you can outgrow anything. I was definitely going to give her a hard time about it on Wednesday. Girls like it when you tease them about something they're good at.

CHAPTER TWO

Next day, I passed Kyle, Forrest, and Matt on their way to the parking lot at lunch, and Forrest held up his hand. "Gabe!"

"You're going the wrong way to lunch," Kyle said. "Cafeteria food sucks." We were all stopped in the hallway, and it was one of those awkward moments where I couldn't tell if he was asking me to come with them.

Forrest made it easy for me. "Let's go. We're getting Mexican."

"Okay," I said, and fell in step.

"This is Matt." Forrest jerked his head toward Matt Chen, like everybody in school didn't know who he was. He was Asian, tall, and big, which was an unusual combo, and the girls loved it, judging by how they tracked him in class.

"You're in fourth-period history, right?" I asked.

Matt nodded. "You're new here?" He had a soft, quiet voice, kind of the opposite of the way he looked.

"Yeah. We moved here in August."

"Where from?" said Forrest, turning into the lot. He clicked his key chain, and the lights flashed on a massive Land Rover.

"White Center. I used to go to Jefferson."

There was a silence, and I saw Forrest and Kyle trade looks. "Really?" said Forrest. "Was that a cool place?"

I grinned. "You don't have to be subtle, dude. It's straight ghetto."

Forrest laughed. "Hey, you said it."

White Center *was* ghetto. We used to call my old school "Destination KCJ," meaning King County Jail. The hood was a weird mix of whites, blacks, Mexicans, and Vietnamese, with families dealing weed out the front and raising chickens out the back.

"Remember that basketball tournament where a guy got knifed a couple years ago?" said Kyle. "That was at Jefferson, right?"

"Yeah, Dre Franklin got stabbed," I said. "He's my boy Devon's brother."

"You *know* him?" said Forrest. He opened the Land Rover, and we all hopped in. As Forrest drove, we talked about the crazy thug from Tacoma who'd knifed Dre right on the court. Dude had a blade strapped to his waist under his basketball shorts. That was the kind of thing that happened at Jefferson.

The Mexican place was small and packed, but the girl quickly got our food—burritos the size of my head—and big paper cups of Coke. It cost ten bucks, which was more than I usually spent on lunch, but I was guessing it was pocket change to those guys.

We set up at a table, and as we were opening our food, Forrest said, "You guys going to Morton's on Friday?"

Kyle dumped salsa on his burrito. "Definitely." He looked at me. "One of our Overlake friends is having a party. You should come."

Forrest said, "Yeah, bring Irina. But watch it, or I'm taking her off your hands."

"Better put a bag over your head if you're going to try that, so you don't scare her off," I said.

Kyle and Matt hooted.

"Nah, she's blind. I mean, she gave *you* her number, right?" Forrest threw back.

Kyle crumpled his wrapper into a ball and said, "Morton's looking for somebody to hook up some party favors. You got any connections at Jefferson? I mean, since all you guys do over there is get high?" He made it sound like a joke, but he and Forrest were both watching me. Matt looked like he wanted to crawl under the table.

Actually, I had all kinds of connections. I could have driven forty minutes and swung by my friend Damon's dad's meth shed, or called my buddy Tim to hook up molly and Oxies, or bought dirt weed by the tire load from the Mexican family on South Street. So yeah, I could hook it up. And I could probably add a rich-kid tax, and they'd never know the difference.

I glanced at Matt, who obviously felt like he was stuck in some after-school special.

"Don't pay attention to him," said Forrest. "He's straight-edge, but he's cool."

Matt rolled his eyes. "You guys are idiots. That shit kills people."

I smiled. I liked these dudes, even Matt. "I'll see," I said.

Kyle said, "Cool. And if you don't bring Irina, my girlfriend's friend wants to meet you."

"Who?" Forrest demanded. "Becky?"

Kyle nodded.

"Lucky fool." Forrest slugged me in the arm.

By the time we got back to school, we'd all traded numbers, and I felt better than I had since I moved.

♠ ♣ ♥ ♦

Wednesday night before Irina's concert, I was like a cartoon character, dropping crap and sweating bullets with my heart beating out of my chest in big valentines. *Why?* I had no idea. I didn't even know the girl! And I'd been out with a million girls.

I think it was that violin. It was sexy that she was so good at something. And yeah, I'm a typical guy. It was also that she wasn't throwing herself at me—at all. In fact, I'd texted her, and she hadn't texted back. So of course I was whipped.

I spent so long getting ready, my mom knew something was up. She peeked in the bathroom at me (I was fooling with my hair) and said, "You have a date, don't you?"

I didn't say no. She squealed and said, "Tell me about her!"

"Nothing. Just some girl." I smashed my cowlick again—stupid thing would never stay down—and pulled at my shirt.

Mom pushed the door open a little more and looked around at the mess of deodorant, gel, mouthwash, and towels. "You look so handsome. She's going to be head over heels for you."

I made a face. "No, she's not. Can I borrow your car?"

"Sure." Mom's eyes were twinkling. "'Love, bittersweet, irrepressible, loosens my limbs and I tremble.' That's Sappho."

I knew it was Sappho. I'd heard it before, every time Mom found a new guy. Mom would go online and look through quote websites for hours, and when she found one she liked, she'd write it down in this cheesy book with an angel on the cover. Once I told her that a quote only counts if you read the book it came from, and she got mad at me. We're not supposed to talk about how we both suck at reading.

Mom disappeared, and a second later she was back with her purse. "Be a gentleman and pay for her food." She handed me the keys and a twenty.

"Thanks." I took the money, but I felt bad. Phil was so stingy, he didn't give Mom enough for any extras. Kyle's offer flew through my head again.

"Have fun!" Mom stood aside to let me down the stairs.

Fun? Weirdly, I was hoping for something more than that, although I wasn't exactly sure what.

♠ ♣ ♥ ♦

The concert was in Fisher Pavilion at Seattle Center, where they hold all the free concerts for Winterfest. I got there early so I could grab a seat in front. I wanted Irina to see me the whole time. My plan was to ask her to get coffee after. I thought she might try to talk about music, so while I was waiting, I looked up a big-time classical music blog (according to Technorati) called *The Rest Is Noise*.

I couldn't concentrate on my phone's tiny screen, so I gave up after reading a blurb about some Chinese dude, Lao Ping, who was rocking the classical music world with his *passionately lyrical performances*. Good enough.

I had a reality-check moment. *Am I seriously memorizing comments about classical music?* Then Irina walked onstage with the rest of the musicians. She was wearing a white button-down shirt and black skirt, very professional-looking and mad hot. As she sat down, she smiled at me, and in that one second she made up for the music homework.

The concert I mostly ignored. Whoever invented the drums did the world a giant favor. But Irina did play awesome, if you like that kind of thing: passionate, fingers flying, bow jumping. Watching her, I wished I was good at something.

I'm not, though. Or if I am, it's stuff that doesn't count: Playing poker. Getting girls' numbers. When I was a kid, skipping rocks. Seriously, that's all I can think of.

The concert went on for a freaking ice age, and the whole time I was getting more and more nervous about what I'd say to Irina, and whether I even had a chance; because after that smile, she didn't really look my way again. In fact, she seemed to be staring at a different part of the audience, and I had this horrible thought that maybe there was some other guy, but I checked and everyone was like sixty.

Finally the concert finished. I waited around, pretending to check out the booklet they gave me, while the audience broke up and drifted out the doors. She'd come through, wouldn't she? I didn't want to seem like I was watching the stage . . .

Then I heard a voice behind me. "Hey, you came."

I whipped around, and she was standing there with her coat on, holding her violin box. I said, "Yeah, you played really good."

"Thanks." She stared at me curiously. Her face was so delicate: thin nose, tilted eyes with light brown lashes, smooth blond hair.

"You want to get a coffee?"

She looked over her shoulder, then back at me. "Okay. A quick one."

"Are you here with someone? Your parents?"

"Yeah, my dad's here. But he's talking with his friends, and he'll probably take a while."

I looked past her at a bunch of older guys in suits standing in a circle. I sure hoped the six-foot-five bulldog-looking one wasn't her dad. "We can go right there if you want." I nodded toward Starbucks at the other end of the pavilion.

"Okay," Irina said. I could see all the other guys watching her as we walked over to Starbucks. Guys think they're sly, but their eyes do this obvious tracking thing. It made me proud.

We got drinks and sat down at one of the rickety metal tables by the stage. Irina pulled back her blond hair and snapped on a rubber band. She did everything fast and confident, even putting back her hair. Her hands were tiny and pretty and . . . man, I had it bad. I wanted to skip the getting-to-know-you and lean in and kiss her perfect mouth.

"You played like Lao Ping. Really intense but lyrical," I said.

She grinned. "Have you been reading Alex Ross's blog? 'Cause it's funny, he said the same thing yesterday."

My face heated up. Why was I so stupid? Of course she read that blog, too. "Yeah," I admitted, fiddling with a straw wrapper on the table.

She gave me a hard look—but not unfriendly. "Gabe, do you really like classical music? Or was this whole thing just a way to get my number?"

Damn. The flush was getting worse. *Called out to the billionth power.* I had a feeling if I lied, she'd see right through me. And besides, I didn't want to lie to her. "No, I'm not really that into it," I mumbled. "But I don't hate it or anything."

She laughed. "I knew it. Thanks for sitting through that whole concert."

"You were good! Seriously! I like classical music if you're playing it."

She gave me a really nice smile, and I could tell she wasn't mad.

"I saw a bunch of your YouTube videos," I said. "You're like a prodigy, huh?"

The smile dropped off her face. "No, I'm not."

"That wasn't you?"

Her cheeks were getting pink. "It was me, but I'm not a prodigy. A prodigy is a genius. *Mozart* was a prodigy."

"Okay, you're not a prodigy. How'd you get so good, though?" I asked her.

She took a sip of coffee. "If you spend six hours a day doing something, you get pretty good at it."

"Six hours a *day?*" I couldn't imagine doing anything for that long, except sleeping.

"Yeah, two years ago I started homeschooling, which means every day I practice for six hours and then study for two hours with a music master."

"That's kind of . . . insane," I said. "What about schoolwork?"

She shrugged. "No offense, but my parents think school in this country is a joke. I have my GED, and I'm going to a music conservatory instead of college anyway, so it doesn't really matter."

I put my elbows on the table. "What do you mean 'school in this country'? What country are you from?"

"Well, I was born here, but I'm Russian."

I looked at her almond eyes and perfect white skin, and yeah, of course she was Russian. That's where all the models came from. "Cool," I said. "So were your parents born in Russia?"

"My mom is from Petersburg, and my dad is second generation, but his dad was from Krasnodar." Irina made her voice deep, with a heavy accent. "Irinushka, ze job of true Rossians ees to breeng great art into ze vorld. Ve understand sorrow and passion, and so ve are ze voice of beauty. Tchaikovsky, Rachmaninov, Pasternak, Barishnikov, Akhmatova . . . Thees are your people."

I cracked up. She sounded exactly like an old Russian dude.

She looked pleased. "That's my grandpa."

"So your job is to bring art into the world?"

She nodded and her eyes got a little gleam, and I saw that she totally believed it. And I believed it, too—she was that good. "That's what Russians do," she said proudly.

A couple sarcastic comments about the *other* things Russians do, like run violent mobs and have screwed-up political systems, jumped into my head, but it's not like I knew that much about it, so I kept my mouth shut. Note to self: don't bash hot girl's country.

"So, what are you into?" she asked, looking at me over her cup. "What kind of work do you want to do?"

It was weird to me that she connected those two questions, like they had something to do with each other. It was depressing that I didn't have an answer for either one. I took a swig of coffee to buy time. *Sorry, no talents, no future, and no plans except finding enough cash to buy a decent car. Feel free to leave whenever.*

"I'm into . . . science. I'm going to be a doctor, probably." *Oh crap, did I really say that?* There should have been a big red lie alarm on my head, flashing like crazy.

She tilted her head to the side and said, "Wow, that's really cool. What kind of doctor?"

"A pediatrician." It was the first thing I thought of.

She looked sort of mushy. "That's so sweet. You love kids?"

I nodded, making my lie alarm explode into pieces, because the truth is, I think kids are noisy little grease monkeys who can screw up a perfectly good day just by being around. At least Jason, my neighbor, can, and he's the only kid I know.

"I do, too. I want to have like ten of them," she confessed.

Any other girl and I swear I would have found a way to end the date right there, but I smiled at her and said, "Me, too," and for half a second I actually meant it, because, in my head, it was somehow connected with getting to sleep with her ten times.

"Russians don't do that, though," she went on. "It's seen as tacky to have more than one or two. But I always wanted a big family, or at least a sister. It's too much pressure, being the only one. It's like your parents don't have anything to focus on except you."

I was an only kid and my mom wasn't too "focused" on me, but I didn't want to admit it. I changed the subject. "So if you're homeschooled, who do you hang out with?"

She gave an awkward laugh. "Nobody, really. My best friend, Anya, moved to New York last year, and when I stopped going to school, I sort of lost touch with people. Besides, there's not that much time left over after violin practice." She paused, and her brown-gold eyes met mine. "And I'm a freak."

"No, you're not," I said.

"How would you know?"

I didn't have an answer for that. She was a music genius, and she was homeschooled. Those two things alone equaled freak.

"Well, then you're a cool, beautiful freak." For a second, I was scared it came out insulting, but she smiled. "You just spend too much time working," I went on. "You're a teenager. You're supposed to have fun." I held her eyes, and she didn't look down like most girls would. "You want to come to a party with me Friday night?"

The second I asked, a bunch of reasons why this was *not* a good idea rushed through my head, such as I wanted to check out this Becky girl who supposedly liked me. And I wanted to keep Irina to myself; I didn't want rich boys scoping her.

"Okay," said Irina. But then her face kind of froze. She stood up.

"What?" I said, turning around.

Damn. The six-foot-five bulldog had broken off from the circle and was marching over. He had those piercing Russian eyes and five o'clock shadow that would break a razor, and he was wearing a black suit. He seriously looked like a Mob boss.

"I'll text you about the party," Irina said quickly. She grabbed her violin and practically jogged toward him.

CHAPTER THREE

Stupid idiot. That's what I was for asking Irina out without making sure the car situation was handled. Turned out Mom needed the car that night. She and a bunch of her middle-aged-going-on-nineteen buddies from White Center had a book club—except, according to Mom, none of them actually read the books. They just got drunk and talked trash about their exes.

Anyway, "book club" was the night of Morton's party, and I was supposed to pick up Irina at her place. The cool thing to do would be to just show up, and hell with what she thought . . . but my ride was one of those messed-up toy cars that Europeans drive. It was fourteen years old. Its bumper was held on by duct tape. I had to squeeze to fit into the seat, because Europeans are midgets. And the car stank like dog, and the upholstery looked like the dog had cheese graters for paws.

Back in White Center, I was kind of a hero for driving it. All my friends called me "Claude the French Pimp" and pretended I ran a call-girl service out of my ride. But in Redmond it was just a piece of crap. And by the way, I didn't buy it; I won it from a meth-head vet in Scrappy's Pool Hall.

I wasn't going within ten miles of Irina in that thing. So it was either make her drive herself, which wasn't an option, because she texted *Pick me up Sat at 8* with her address, or rent a car. The problem was cash. I'd just cleaned out my savings buying a new laptop and I had only fifty bucks left. A decent rental plus insurance and gas would easily be seventy. I also needed extra money in case Irina wanted to go out after the party. There was a place I could generally find some, but it wasn't exactly risk-free. Still, it was the only way I knew to get quick cash, aside from stealing.

♠ ♣ ♥ ♦

The biggest White Center poker game was in Fausto Gonzales's shed. I'd learned about the game from his son, Miguel, one of my buddies from middle school. Miguel and I used to play Hold'em for quarters in study hall, and one time he invited me to help out when his dad was hosting a tournament. Our job was to run beer back and forth from the big fridge in the house. At the end of the tourney, Mr. Gonzales let me play a round, and I won fifty bucks. I'd been playing on and off ever since.

On Wednesday night, I drove to the Gonzaleses' old brown ranch on Roxbury. They had a fierce Dobie, but he knew my smell, and when he saw me, he barked only once, just saying hello. I went around back, past their chicken coop, to the little beat-up poker shed. There was a crack of light around the door; open for business. I was looking to turn the fifty in my pocket into at least a hundred.

I knocked and said into the crack, "It's Gabe, Miguel's friend."

There was a scraping sound, and Mr. Gonzales opened the door, his round face beaming. He was a real dapper dude, with one of those pencil mustaches, and he always wore nice threads. "Gabe! Where you been? Miguel told me you moved."

"Yeah, we live in Redmond now."

Mr. Gonzales whistled. "Your ma hit the lottery or what?"

I smiled. "Not exactly. Is Miguel around?"

"He's off with his girlfriend somewhere." Mr. Gonzales rolled his eyes. "He thinks he's in love. Come in. We got Tony and Marquis here already, and a couple guys are coming from Seattle. They're bringing a whale."

"Yeah? Too bad I don't have a bigger bankroll." I walked in, feeling good to be back in familiar digs. It was real basic in there: just a mini-fridge, table, space heater, and a lightbulb hanging on a frayed cord. There were marks on the walls where tools had hung until a few months ago, when some dude from Tacoma lost big and decided to grab a shovel and get even.

I raised a hand to Marquis and Tony, who were at the table with beers. Tony was shuffling, flicking the cards in perfect arches. He was half-Italian, half-Irish, and he lived up to the stereotypes: he could outtalk and outdrink anybody.

"What's up?" Marquis greeted me. He was a young brotha with a shaved head, and he kept a low profile. All the newbies underestimated him because they thought poker wasn't a black man's game.

I knew better. Those two were a slick team and had a bucket of tricks to use on whales and other targets: mirror rings, marked decks, and even some contraption that Marquis kept up his sleeve for grabbing aces. They'd been kicked out of Tulalip and all the other Native casinos, and they claimed to be blackballed in Vegas, too.

"How much you want in chips, Gabe?" asked Mr. Gonzales.

"Just fifty. I was looking for a low-stakes game," I said. "That's why I came early."

Mr. Gonzales looked at the guys. "We're putting the minimum bet at a hundred when the whale gets here, but if you want to squeeze in a game with Tony and Marquis, it's up to them."

"Sure," said Marquis. "I could use an extra fifty bucks." He winked at me.

I pulled out a folding chair and sat down. "No offense, but . . ." I looked at Marquis's sleeves.

"You're paranoid. We always play straight with you, kid." He shook out his sleeves and rolled them up.

"Yeah, well, it never hurts to check," I said. "Tony, let me see that deck."

Tony looked annoyed, but he handed over the cards.

"All right. Let's play," I said after thumbing through the deck. I couldn't really tell if it was marked, but we had a code of honor: friends of Mr. G.'s couldn't cheat other friends of Mr. G.'s. Everybody else was fair game.

Tony was the button, and he dealt the hole cards quickly. I had a solid read on him—he was a chip clicker—but not on Marquis. Marquis wouldn't have blinked during a game if you stabbed his foot. I started with a nine of hearts and a three of diamonds. We posted the blinds and got rolling. When an eight of hearts came up,

I got interested, but I still checked. Then a seven of hearts turned, and I went ahead and threw some more money in the pot.

"So, what's your mother doing in Redmond?" Tony asked.

I frowned at my cards. "She has a new boyfriend. A real bastard."

Tony shook his head. "A gorgeous woman like her, that's a shame." I gave him a grossed-out glance. I knew guys thought my mom looked good, but I didn't like hearing about it. Especially not from Tony.

"You like it out there?" asked Marquis.

"It's cool." I pushed some money into the pot. "I met a girl."

He looked up. "Oh, listen to him. He met a girl. You like her, kid. I can hear it."

I couldn't help it; I smiled. Then there was the sound of a car on gravel outside, and Mr. Gonzales froze for a second, then hopped to the door and started gesturing with his arms. The *real* money had arrived.

"Hang on, man. Let us finish the hand," Marquis said, and threw down a sweet flush.

I sighed and set down my three of a kind; so did Tony. Marquis looked smug as he swept the chips into his pile. At least it was only fifty. I'd lost more than that to Marquis, although he'd lost his share to me, too.

As I stood up, Tony pulled another deck out of his bag and switched it with the one we'd been using. Marquis was on his knees, tinkering with something under the table. Mr. Gonzales whispered a password question through the door, stalling for time. Everybody was set to go whaling.

"Peace, guys," I said.

"Don't be a stranger, now." Marquis stood up and put his hands in his pockets.

Mr. Gonzales opened the door, and three guys trailed in: two regulars and the whale, who turned out to be a heavy Asian dude. He looked a little drunk already. I nodded at him, said thanks to Mr. G., and took off.

♠ ♣ ♥ ♦

I wasn't thrilled about losing at poker, but I knew it was a long shot. And I wasn't out of options for finding cash. I'd planned on hooking up Kyle's friend, anyway.

I did some quick math, texted Kyle to see how much his friend needed, and drove to meet Missy Peterson at the Red Robin in Burien on Thursday night. Missy was like a sister to me. She'd lived near us in White Center, and her dad had dated my mom for six months, which was a record for both of them. Her older brother, Tim, was a small-time dealer, and Missy did some of his deliveries.

Missy was already at Red Robin when I got there, and she squeezed the breath out of me in a hug. Even though she was clean, she looked like an early-stage junkie, probably from being raised on Cap'n Crunch and Frito sandwiches. She had that glow-in-the-dark skin, scrawny ten-year-old-boy legs, and hair that had been through so many bottles of dye, it looked like orange fur. But at that moment, I was so happy to see her, I swear she looked beautiful.

"Hey, woman!" I hugged her back.

She ran her tongue over her front tooth, which had gotten chipped in a fight, and examined me. "It's good to see you. You look good." We sat down in a booth, and she put her elbows on the table.

"So, how are you doing over there?" She said *there* like a dirty word. Missy had big scorn for yuppies. She felt they'd taken over Seattle.

"It's okay. They're all crazy rich, but they're not jerks or anything. Except this corporate tool my mom's dating."

We shared a look. Missy knew my mom; I knew her dad. It wasn't clear which one was the bigger flake. Her dad was definitely meaner, though.

"It's so weird that she's going for a suit. That's not her style," Missy said.

I shook my head. "I know. I don't get it."

"Maybe she decided the guys she's always attracted to turn out bad, so she's trying to break the mold?"

"Maybe," I said, "but this mold is worse." I couldn't believe I was actually saying that about a dude with a job and no drug habit, but it was true.

Missy wrinkled her nose. "Sorry. That sucks."

"How's your man?" I asked. She'd been dating Jake Reese for so long, they were practically married. He was already out of high school, a complete stoner, but a very nice guy with good taste in music. He did lawns for a living.

She got a funny smile. "He's good. Same old, same old. You know Jake."

"Tell him what's up for me." I hoped someday I could smile like that about somebody after being together a couple years. I always got bored after a few months, though. Just bad luck, I hoped, and not a sign that I was crap for relationships.

Missy changed the subject. "I brought your stuff. Tim's giving you a fat discount, by the way."

"Tell him thanks."

"He wants to know, is this going to be a regular thing?"

"I don't know. I'll see how much I get for this batch."

Missy gave me a stern look. "Don't get caught, and don't dip, okay?"

I could understand why she was worried; Tim had been dipping lately, which everyone knows is death for a dealer—not that anyone could talk to him about it without starting a fight.

"You know I don't roll like that," I said. It was true. Weed was nice, and so was e, but not too much of either. Meth I had tried twice and loved, but I didn't touch the stuff because of how *much* I'd loved it. Plus I'd seen what raving assholes it turned people into.

We chilled awhile longer, talked, ate some fries, and then did the deal out by Missy's car. I gave her a big hug good-bye and promised to call soon. When I left, I felt good. Hanging with Missy grounded me, reminded me that there were solid people I could count on, people I didn't have to prove anything to.

I texted Kyle on the drive home. I didn't mention that I was making fifteen dollars' profit on every pill—just gave him the price and set up the handoff for lunch at a restaurant the next day.

I felt bad for a minute. Friends aren't supposed to make money off friends. But really, I was doing them a favor.

♠ ♣ ♥ ♦

The night of the party, I drove to the Redmond car rental, paid the annoying under-twenty-five charge, picked up my ride (a boring but decent Taurus), and mapped Irina's house on my phone.

I knew it was a lot of trouble to go to for a girl. But somehow, in my head, getting with Irina had become a mission. We'd been talking on the phone and texting, and she was different than other girls. I could tell she didn't put out easy. If she slept with me, she'd mean it, and it would be . . . something.

Plus I'd be a hero to the guys.

I figured it might take a while. It's not that I don't have confidence; most girls take three weeks, a month tops, to crack, and those are the ones playing hard to get. But I was ready for something real. I had this bad thought sometimes, that I might never know what it was like to love a girl.

I headed down 180th Avenue through a nice neighborhood, and I started noticing that with each street, the houses were getting bigger and farther apart. Then, duh, it clicked—the girl was beyond loaded—and I pulled up outside her place.

Back in White Center, *rich* was having a big house that looked exactly like all the other big houses on the Burien golf course. The rich-people houses in this hood looked more like government buildings. Irina's place was a redbrick beast with white pillars and a football field for a lawn. The walkway looked like somebody scrubbed it with a toothbrush, and the bushes around the house were clipped in perfect circles.

I rang the bell, thinking maybe a servant would open the door. But it was Irina who did. She was smiling.

I went to hug her—I thought I could at least do that—and then I about jumped out of my skin. There was someone behind her, a thin blond lady staring at me with laser-beam eyes.

"Hello," she said.

Irina said, "Mom, this is Gabe. Gabe, this is my mom."

"You can call me Mrs. Petrova," the woman said in a smoker's voice. I could see where Irina got her looks. Her mom was hot, even though she had to be like forty. And she looked high-class, with rocks in her ears and black everywhere else. "Irina, invite your friend in for some tea."

"Mom, we'll be late."

Mrs. Petrova tossed her head and walked away, obviously expecting us to follow.

Irina sighed. "You want some tea? It'll only take a minute. Mom is just going to make sure you're European, rich, and artistic."

My eyes must have popped, because she smiled and said, "Don't worry—I'm kidding. Sort of."

Crap. Of course I wasn't going to pass the parent test. The whole thing was a setup. But I put on my game face and followed Irina through the house, taking in the spindly polished-tooth-pick furniture; puffy, long, cut-in-half couches; black baby grand; and some angry-looking women staring out of gold frames on the walls.

Irina led me through *that* room to a dining room that was a little more comfortable, with a long table and wood chairs and lots of windows. "This is the breakfast room," she said.

I was so out of my element, it was sick.

A minute later, Mrs. Petrova came in, carrying a tray with a silver pot and three tiny cups. She waved at the table. "Sit down." Irina and I sat with a seat between us, and Mrs. Petrova poured tea and passed around cups. No sugar, no milk, just little floating lemons. Nasty.

She sat down across from us, took a sip of her tea, and stared at me. "Irina tells me you like ballet?"

So Irina wasn't above lying. *Good to know.* "Yes, ma'am."

"You prefer—"

"He likes the Kirov Ballet the best, Mom," Irina cut in. "His favorite choreographer is Petipa. And his favorite dancer is Nureyev. Any more questions?"

Her mom looked back and forth between us, eyes narrowed. "Are you joking with me?"

I shook my head.

"Nureyev is really your favorite?"

"Yes, she's amazing!" I said.

Mrs. Petrova's forehead crunched into a glare. "Bah," she said, disgusted, and got up and stalked out. A second later, she poked her head back in and pointed threateningly at Irina. "*You.*" Then she disappeared again.

Irina was giggling. "Rudolph Nureyev is a man, you idiot."

"I don't even think of ballet dancers as male," is what popped out of my stupid mouth. Irina looked at me like I just said I didn't know how to read. But it was true: I seriously didn't know a guy in his right mind who would try ballet.

She stood. "Come on. We should leave before my mom changes her mind about letting me go. She danced for the Kirov Ballet. Not knowing Nureyev is like not knowing George Washington or something."

"Your mom's a ballerina?"

"Oh yeah."

I was thrilled to get out of there, although I was starting to wish I'd sold some more pills and rented a Ferrari. We got in the Taurus and pulled away, and with every block we got farther away from Irina's house, I felt a little bit of my cool coming back. I turned up the stereo and merged onto the I-5, following the directions Kyle gave me.

After we'd been driving a few minutes, I asked, "So, how come you ran away so fast when you saw your dad coming the other night?"

"If you knew my dad, you wouldn't ask that," Irina said.

I gave her a sideways look. I didn't like the sound of that. "What, he doesn't like you talking to guys?"

"He would have given you a hard time."

"Why?"

"You weren't wearing a dress shirt to a concert, your hair is kind of long, all that stuff." She waved a hand.

I ran a hand over my hair. "What are you talking about? It's like two inches!"

"Yeah, but it's messy."

I frowned. I worked hard to get my hair looking like that.

"Don't worry about my dad," Irina said. "He's not here now, is he?"

No, he wasn't. But the dude gave me a spooky feeling, like if I got any closer with his daughter, I'd be dealing with him.

CHAPTER FOUR

When we got to Morton's house, Irina and I went up the front steps, where some guys were sitting, smoking menthols. Kyle was one of them, and he gave me a fist bump as we walked in, and checked out Irina way too obviously.

Inside, it was more like a bad rave than a high school party. Everybody was rolling with their candy rings, the 'tronic was pumping, and you could smell the weed and liquor. A bunch of people were dancing, and one girl in a shiny pink go-go outfit was trancing against the speaker—except it was only about four feet tall, so she looked silly. On the floor, a bunch of kids with a jar of Vicks had a back rub train going on.

As me and Irina walked by, somebody said, "Gabe!" and suddenly everyone was saying hi or reaching up for fist bumps or whatever. It was pretty nice, actually, to have that happen in front of Irina. Kyle must have spread the word that I'd connected the e. Well, I'd take it. Irina didn't need to know why.

"You want a drink?" I offered, and Irina shrugged, so we headed to the bar in the kitchen. A dude playing bartender made us some top-shelf jungle juice, and we found a spot to lean against the wall.

Irina's expression was hard to read. "Are these your friends?" she asked, looking at the back rub train.

"No," I said honestly. "I haven't lived here that long, and I'm still kind of getting to know people."

She gave me a curious look. "Where did you come from before?"

"Over by West Seattle."

"What, like Burien?"

"White Center," I muttered.

She said thoughtfully, "White Center? That makes sense. There's something about the way you talk . . ." I looked at her, and she paused. "I mean, it's just a little different than I'm used to."

"Oh, sorry, is this better?" I said in an English accent, and she laughed. I told her, "I'm actually from New York. We moved to White Center when I was in fourth grade. So you're probably hearing leftover East Coast."

"Yeah, you say a's different."

I didn't answer, because I saw some girls coming toward us from across the room. One of them was Kyle's girlfriend, Erin, and she had three other girls with her: a redhead and two brunettes lined up in a hottie brigade.

Irina saw them and set her drink on a bookshelf. I didn't have a chance to ask her what was up, because the girls were on us.

"Irina!" said the redhead, and gave her a cheek kiss. "I haven't seen you in forever!"

One of the brunettes leaned in for a cheek kiss, too, and they kind of pulled Irina away into a girl knot. Well, that was good, I guessed. I wanted her to feel welcome. I wondered how they knew each other, anyway. From when Irina went to regular school?

Erin and the last brunette moved in on me. Erin asked, "Hey, Gabe, have you met Becky Philman?"

She knew I hadn't.

Becky smiled and said, "Hi," in a soft voice. I looked at Irina really quick, because I felt like there was a big red sign on my forehead, "Checking Out Another Girl," but the other two were walking away with her. *Girls are so damn crafty.*

"Hey," I said to Becky. "I've seen you at school." I *had* seen her; she was hard to miss—long brown hair; light blue eyes; curvy in the best way.

"Yeah, you have English third period, and I'm in chemistry next door." Then she blushed, and man, I kind of fell for that. It's hard to fake a blush.

"How do you like Stevens?" I asked, because I knew he taught chemistry that period, and I'd heard he was a monster.

Becky started telling me about his horrible quiz policy, and Erin said, "Oh, I think Kyle needs me," and melted away. The jungle juice was pretty potent, and Becky was one of those soft, nice girls who look at you like you're a king, and I started to really enjoy myself. She wasn't hard to talk to, and I felt back in my game. I didn't have to go renting cars to impress this girl.

There was a break in the conversation, and Kyle and Erin walked by, wrapped around each other.

"Kyle thinks you're cool," Becky informed me, like she was giving me extremely good news.

I raised my eyebrows. "I think *you're* cool."

She knocked back whatever she had in that red plastic cup and touched my wrist lightly—an invitation.

I wanted to so badly, I actually took a step after her. But then I stopped. I wasn't *that* drunk. I'd brought Irina here, where she barely knew anybody except a few girls who were running interference for their friend. It would be a jerk move to take someone else into a back room. Besides, I'd already put a lot of effort into Irina, and going off with Becky would mess that up.

I was just buzzed enough to tell the truth. "I can't. I brought somebody. But I wish I could. I like you." Becky turned flame red and I felt so bad, I made it worse. "I mean, I'm not saying you want to do anything, I'm not conceited like that, but—"

Becky squeezed my arm. "It's okay. You're doing the right thing." Then she disappeared.

I tossed back the rest of my juice and decided it was time to find Irina. Because I was having serious thoughts of going after Becky and telling her hold on, I made a mistake, let's hit that closet. *Something good had better happen with Irina to make up for this.* Where was she, anyway?

I pushed through the crowd and almost knocked into Forrest. He was yelling something at Matt, and they both looked fired up. Forrest grabbed my arm. "Gabe! Where would India be without British colonization?"

I had no idea what he was talking about, but it didn't matter, because Matt threw back, "This fool is trying to say colonization was a good thing! Forget the dead bodies in the sugar fields!"

"That was a tragedy, okay?" snapped Forrest. "I'm not saying it wasn't. What I'm saying is that India's jumping into the first world because they made the best of a bad situation. They looked at the British system. They said, 'This works. Let's use it.' And now look at their growth rate in GDP!"

"You're a white dude!" Matt said. "Of course you—"

"Ad hominem!" shouted Forrest.

I clapped them both on the backs, and Forrest sloshed his beer a little. "I'm going to leave you two alone," I said. They were like professors posing as people my age. Was everybody at Claremont like this, or just my new friends?

I wandered back through the party—people were definitely flying now—and guess what? Irina wasn't too hard to find at all. She was in the middle of a circle of rowers and lacrosse players, who were all pure undiluted first-class assholes, if you asked me. She was grinning and her eyes were sparkling, and she must have been saying something funny, because all the guys were laughing.

I walked right up to the group, edged in, and stared at her, like, *What?*

She winked. *Winked!* "Hey, Gabe," she said, and went back to talking about whatever. Then Pete Winters, who's one of those genetic freaks with a Superman body and Polo-model face, put his arm around her!

That was it. I shoved through the admirers and said in her ear, "This is boring. You want to go?"

She looked at me, looked at Pete, and gave me this wicked smile like she knew exactly what I was worried about. Then she said, "Yeah, let's get out of here."

I admit it was a pretty great moment seeing those dudes' faces as we left. But I was stinging. Leave a hot girl for one second and she gets attacked.

"You seem to make friends pretty quick," I said the second we were in the car.

She closed her seat belt. "I know those guys from middle school. Anyway, I could say the same for you."

I took off down the road. "It's not my fault she was hitting on me."

Irina laughed. "You looked like you really minded."

Dang. I didn't know she'd been watching. *Better change the subject.* "It's still early. You want to check out Marymoor Park?" I'd heard it was a good place to take girls.

"You mean Hookup Park?" she teased. "I'm kind of tired, actually. I need to get home."

I frowned. "I never said anything about hooking up. I just feel like walking."

"Uh-huh, sure." Irina paused, then said gently, "Gabe, I'm not into head games. I'm going to be honest with you. Nothing is going to happen between us. You should have gone for that girl, if you wanted to."

I stared straight ahead, trying to hide my shock. Finally I said, "Why is nothing going to happen between us?"

"I'm not your type."

I was starting to get mad. I pressed down harder on the gas. "How do you know what my type is?"

"I guess I don't, but I'm pretty sure I'm not it." She started ticking off on her fingers. "I'm not 'cool.' I'm into stuff like classical music. I'm not going to have sex with you."

I stopped her right there. "So you're not attracted to me."

"I didn't say that. I'm just not having sex until I'm married."

I almost crashed the car. "What? Who even does that?"

"I do."

"Why?"

"A few reasons."

My mind was racing. It had to be religion. She was probably wearing one of those rings. A few girls I knew had them, and it meant they were engaged to God or their dad or something. I glanced down.

She saw me looking and held out her hand. "I'm not wearing a purity ring. I'm not Protestant. I'm Orthodox."

"You're Jewish?" I felt like an idiot. I didn't think of Jewish people as blond.

She smiled. "No, Russian Orthodox. It's Christian. And we don't wear purity rings. But yeah, one of my reasons for waiting is my religion."

"What are the others?"

She looked out the window. "You'll think it's stupid."

"No, I won't," I said. "Tell me."

She took a breath. "I want a relationship that's deep. Like the best music. It takes a long time to build that. In America, every-thing is on the surface. People think they're in love if they want to have sex with someone. I want to love with my mind and soul. And I want it to last my whole life, to have one great love—not a bunch of experiments. So I'm waiting."

I snorted. "In America? Come on, you're telling me Russians only have deep, meaningful love affairs? I don't think so." *Oops. Shouldn't have said that.* I looked over, and sure enough, she looked annoyed. I tried to backpedal. "Never mind. Anyway, you don't have to love somebody to have sex with them. You can just like them. Or you can even just want them. It doesn't have to be all serious."

Irina made a sound with her tongue, a Russian sound. "That's cheap. And it diminishes people who do it."

"Diminishes? How?" I said.

"They're using themselves up."

"Sex isn't like money. You don't spend it and use it up," I said. "There's always more."

Irina said quietly, "No, it's not like money. But a person can get used up. They can get so that sex is just a physical act for them, like eating."

Now, that was a weird thing to say. Because honestly, I thought sex *was* sort of like eating. You get hungry, you eat, then you're full. At least, that was the only way it ever felt to me. I wondered again what it would be like to have sex with a girl I loved. But there was no way I was admitting that to Irina.

"You're not going to find a guy who'll wait," I told her. "And you're definitely not going to find a guy who's a virgin, if that's what you want. Unless he's a loser."

She rolled her eyes at me. "You don't even know what a loser is. It takes a man to wait."

An image of Phil the Toolbox flashed into my head.

"Besides," she said, "even if he's not a virgin, I'll make him wait at least a few years while we're engaged."

"He'll cheat on you," I said confidently.

"And that," she said softly, "is why you and I have no future."

I felt my face heating up. "I'm not a cheater!" It was a lie. I had cheated on the only two serious girlfriends I ever had. Quite a few times.

Irina said, "Sorry. I didn't mean to be insulting."

I glanced at her, and she looked so beautiful with her cool stare and pale skin that I wanted to kiss her right there and make her admit she was wrong; we did have something. "Are you attracted to me?" I demanded, because I wanted a straight answer.

"Of course I am. You're ridiculously hot. And I think you have a good heart, although I can't tell for sure."

I felt a little better.

She went on. "But you seem like sort of a player, and anyway, I'm attracted to a lot of people."

Man, this girl could put her spike heel through a guy's heart and grind it in. The problem with her was that she was too used to calling the shots. She needed a guy who didn't let her boss him around.

"Let's just be friends, then," I said, really cool. "Are you allowed to do that? Be friends with a guy?"

She looked surprised. "You really want to be my friend?"

I nodded.

"Okay. I would like that." She sounded happy. *Good move.*

I pulled up outside her house and had a sudden thought. "You don't have a boyfriend or anything, do you?"

"No."

"Are you sure?"

"I'm sure," she said, reaching for the door handle. "Anyway, why do you care, if you just want to be friends?"

"I don't want some Russian dude trying to shoot me."

She giggled. "Other than my dad, no Russian dude is going to try to shoot you."

That was sort of scary.

"Okay, friend. See you later," I said as she climbed out.

She grinned at me. "See you later, Gabe."

I watched her walk into her palace. The princess would go up into her tower and brush her long blond hair. I'd figure out a way to climb up it.

CHAPTER FIVE

After Morton's party, I was "the Man." Nothing like having drug connects and leaving with a pretty girl to build status. The athletes were friendly to me, and Kyle and Forrest kept asking me to lunch and to hang out after school. Matt wasn't sure about me, I could tell, but he was a nice dude and didn't seem to mind that I came along.

The three of them had been tight since elementary. Kyle was the ace; he knew what to say to make people feel good about themselves, but not in a kiss-ass way. And he always seemed to be having a good time, or about to have one.

And Forrest didn't give a shit—about anything. I think he had some messed-up family stuff going on, not that he'd ever talk about it. He was skinny, with dark brown curly hair, and somehow he made his Diesel look as if it came from a pile at Goodwill. He had a wicked edge and liked to shock people, which could be very funny.

Matt was deep into computer science and quiet, except when he was arguing with Forrest. He would have been a computer geek if he wasn't such a good rower. When the rest of us started talking about partying, he'd kind of disappear, or open a book, or check his phone. But he never gave us a hard time. I respected him.

Every day, we'd pile into Kyle's or Forrest's truck and get lunch, usually with a few girls, like Erin and Becky. I think Becky liked me even more after I said I couldn't hook up with her.

One day as we were heading to the parking lot, Kyle said, "Gabe, can you drive? My tank's on E."

My brain stalled for a second. Then I thought, *Fine*. I grinned at him. "You really want me to drive?"

"What are you laughing at?"

"Nothing. Come on." I led the way to my junk heap, which I always parked in the back lot so no one would see it. Their eyes were bugging before I even opened the door. I swept out my arm. "Ladies first."

Erin giggled. "Um . . . are you serious? Will we even fit?"

"Maybe in the trunk," I said.

Kyle chuckled. "That is the worst piece of crap I have seen in my life. Do you seriously drive this thing?"

I shrugged. "I don't have a rich mommy and daddy to buy me a Porsche. Besides, I like my car. It has personality." Inside I was holding my breath. Would they buy it?

They did. They thought it was funny. "Yeah, it does have personality," said Forrest. "It's a pissed-off old man. A dwarf war vet."

"Actually, I won it in a pool game from a vet," I told them, and that sealed it: now they thought the car was cool.

"Yeah, but we're not going to fit. Let's take my car," said Forrest. So we did. I was relieved. Just another reminder that if you act confident, people will swallow anything.

On the way to the restaurant, Kyle gave a fake cough. "Announcement. My parents just told me they're going to Sonoma in two weeks. Second weekend in October, the house is ours."

Forrest whooped. "Party?"

Kyle shook his head. "Nah, did you see how bad they destroyed Morton's place? I'm thinking a small get-together. Just us." He looked at Erin. "And maybe some more of your friends."

Forrest smirked at me over his shoulder. Erin's friends were straight Victoria's Secret.

Kyle punched me on the arm. "Hook up some supplies?"

I didn't answer for a second. It was the third time he'd asked since the last party. On one hand, I had nothing against people getting high. On the other hand, I'd spent plenty of time around the tweakers in White Center, and I knew twenty-five-year-olds who looked fifty, with their nasty rotting teeth and caved-in cheeks and jonesing ways. I'm not saying e is meth, but that gateway crap is real.

But I needed the cash. We were dropping ten bucks a day on lunch, going out sometimes after school, seeing movies . . . Anyway, it's not really dealing if you're just hooking up friends.

"Sure," I said.

"You can bring a friend if you want." He gave me a look and I knew he meant Irina, but he wasn't saying it in front of Becky. Kyle had my back.

"Nah, I'll come alone." I didn't want to scare off Irina with the drugs. I'd been working on her, and I thought I might be getting somewhere. We were hanging out that night, actually. We'd been text-battling over which was better: music with lyrics or music without. She wanted a standoff. I couldn't wait. She was cool; salty as hell, always talking smack. I actually did like her as a friend, although of course I wanted more.

We got to the restaurant, and ordered food and sodas. Becky sat next to me in the brown puffy booth, and Erin kept trying to get us talking the whole time. It's weird how girls are always trying to hook each other up. But I was a little zoned out, thinking about which tracks to play for Irina. KRS One? The Roots? Maybe something old-school, like Bob Dylan?

Then Erin said, "It's going to be great at Kyle's. Small parties are better than big ones." She looked right at me, then at Becky. You couldn't miss her meaning.

Becky turned pink and said in a soft voice, "I like small parties, too."

Suddenly I had pictures of big fancy beds and this sweet girl and me with practically a whole house to ourselves. "Yeah, me, too," I told her.

Erin smiled and took a sip of her Coke.

♠ ♣ ♥ ♦

No way was I going to rent a car just to drive to Irina's house that night, so I parked the junk-mobile half a block away and walked. Irina's mom answered the door. Her blond hair was pulled back, and she was wearing a white sweater and a long black skirt. She didn't even say hi, just, "Follow me."

I looked around, but Irina wasn't coming to save me.

Mrs. Petrova waved her hand. "Come!"

I followed her through the baby-grand room, down a hall, and into another big room, all white: white chairs, white couch, white vases, with a big black-and-white striped rug. It made me paranoid about my shoes. Mrs. Petrova sat on the couch and patted the cushion next to her. "Sit."

I had a sudden horrible thought that maybe she was one of those bored housewives who are into younger guys, and this was going to be like a bad movie, and Irina would walk in right when her mom was pushing me down on the sofa.

Maybe that wouldn't be so bad . . . But Mrs. Petrova picked up a remote, and I realized I was being an idiot. She clicked it, there was a whirring sound, and a screen came down from the ceiling.

"Nureyev," said Mrs. Petrova. *"Le Corsaire."* She pointed the remote.

There were two people in a desert, a guy and a girl, practically naked. They danced for a while, but the guy was so smooth and powerful, you almost didn't notice the girl. She was more like a prop for his moves. Then she danced away and it was just him, and he went crazy. I mean, I never knew a human body could do that. He was spinning so fast, I thought for sure he'd wipe out, but he just kept going. Then he leaped like a deer, over and over. I had to admit, dude was strong.

Mrs. Petrova was watching me. "You see?"

"Yeah, he's really good," I said.

"He is better than good. He is the best," she said sternly. She hit "Stop" and turned to look at me. "Where are your parents from?"

Uh-oh. This was turning out bad after all. "New York?"

She shook her head impatiently. "What is your heritage? What country do your grandparents or your great-grandparents come from?"

This was a crappy question if I ever heard one. *Well, ma'am, I don't know who my father is, so I couldn't tell you where his parents are from, and my mom doesn't know her dad, so I couldn't tell you where he's from, but I'm pretty sure my grandma's from Rochester.*

"I'm Irish," I said. Everybody has some Irish in them.

She squinted at me. "What were your grades on your last report card?"

What kind of bold-ass question was that? She didn't deserve an honest answer. "All As," I said, looking straight at her.

"Really? And what—"

"Mom! How long has Gabe been here?" Irina was standing in the doorway, looking mad. And hot. She was wearing light blue jeans and a white long-sleeved shirt about an inch away from tight.

"I showed him Nureyev," Mrs. Petrova said. "For the first time."

Irina huffed. "Sorry, Gabe. Come on."

I got up and followed her.

"Do *not* close your door!" Mrs. Petrova called after us.

Irina blushed and didn't answer. On the way up the stairs, which were as wide as two normal staircases, she said, "Was it *Le Corsaire*? That's her favorite."

"Yeah. That guy is a serious dancer."

She smiled at me over her shoulder. "Yes, he is." Then we were on the landing, and she led me a few doors down to her room. She left the door open like her mom said.

I looked around. A bedroom can tell you a lot about a person. And Irina's said hard-core musician. There was no rug, just a wooden floor, a four-poster bed with a puffy white comforter, and lace curtains on the windows. There were three metal stands, all with music on them, and two violin boxes, both lying open. The framed pictures on the wall were obviously real paintings. One was—big surprise—a violin. The other was a sad-looking lady staring at her hand.

On the other wall some religious pictures were set up on a dresser with candles. They looked old-fashioned and different, not like the yellow-haired Jesus pictures you see in Walmart, or the Catholic ones with hearts and knives.

A bookshelf took up the rest of the wall. I gave it a closer look, because I thought the books inside might tell me something about Irina. *The Prodigy: A Biography of William James Sidis, America's Greatest Child Prodigy. Mozart: A Life in Music. Life of Sir William Rowan Hamilton.*

"Are these about famous musicians?" I asked, touching the back of one.

She shook her head. "Child prodigies. Who's going first?" She opened a cabinet door on the bottom of the bookshelf, and there was the phattest sound system I'd seen in my life, not counting the ones behind glass in Best Buy.

"You," I said. "So why do you have all those books about child prodigies, if you're not one?" She *was* a prodigy; I knew it.

She sighed. "Because my parents really, really wanted me to be one. And they bought this *shit* to motivate me. But it didn't work. Because I'm not that good!"

I held up my hands. It was kind of strange to hear her curse. "Whoa, sorry. That's kind of crazy they did that."

She shrugged. "It's a whole culture. There are music parents, and math parents, and sports parents . . . My parents did the music thing, because that's what I was good at. There's this one guy? An ex-piano prodigy? He lives in New York now, and he has a Steinway suspended from his ceiling by chains, like the sword of Damocles."

"That's pretty weird," I said.

"Yeah, well, he's onto something." She crouched and fiddled with some dials on the sound system.

"So they made you play even though you didn't want to?"

"It's complicated." She paused. "I did want to. I mean, I *do* want to. I like playing. It's just—I'm not as good as I should be by this point. They really only let me play solo with Microsoft because my dad's the boss."

"Who cares? I mean, so what if you're not a prodigy? I saw you play, and you kick ass. Not that many people kick that much ass at the violin."

"You'd be surprised," she said. "That was true when I was six. But a lot of people play as well as I do now."

I looked around for a place to sit. There were no chairs, so I dropped to the floor and leaned against her bed. "Isn't the violin like a group instrument? Shouldn't it be a good thing that other people can play like you?"

She gave me a funny look. "Yeah, I guess." She turned back to her cabinet. "Okay. This is Tchaikovsky's 1812 Overture. Do you know it?" I shook my head. She put it on and scooted back until she was sitting next to me.

I closed my eyes and looked very serious. The music was fine— if you can stand classical music. "Very powerful," I murmured.

She hit me.

I opened my eyes and smiled at her. "Incredible violins."

"Be quiet and listen!"

I listened. And you know what? I just don't like classical.

When it finished, she said, "Well?"

"No offense, but it sounded like a rip-off of the *Star Wars* soundtrack. I'm totally winning this bet."

She shook her head, smiling. "It's not a bet. It's a contest."

"Contests are a form of bet," I told her. "My turn. This is old-school, but maybe the best rap of all time." I pulled out my phone, connected it to the sound, and put on "Dear Mama" by Tupac.

We listened quietly while Pac laid out what it's really like growing up in the ghetto with no dad. You can hear in his voice that he's for real; he went through this stuff and feels strong about it.

I looked at Irina to see if she liked it, and she was staring out the window, looking sad. I skipped ahead to some Velvet Underground, which was calmer and smoother.

"Why did you turn it off?" demanded Irina.

"Because I'm not trying to make you depressed." The Underground's steady beat pumped through the room.

"It's okay to feel sad about something that *is* sad."

I grabbed her hand and pulled her up. "Yeah, but that wasn't really what I was going for. Come on, let's dance."

"I can't dance to this."

"Sure you can. You're a musician—you can dance to anything." I pulled her close and started kidding around, swaying with her, but suddenly it wasn't a joke. Her hands tightened around my back and she looked up, and I could see straight through her eyes. She was sweet and excited. I was about to kiss her, but she took a breath and moved back a little. She set her hands around my waist, and we both lightened up, and yeah, she could dance.

"You have rhythm," I said in her ear.

"So do you," she said. Then, after a minute, "So, why do you like that Tupac song so much?" She was trying to put it light, but it was a serious question.

"I don't know, he's got passion."

"Can you relate to what he's talking about?"

"What, about having no dad?" I'd told her it was just me and my mom, but I was hoping she wouldn't ask any more about it.

"No, just . . . the way he lives."

I thought about how far away from her house I had to park. "A little bit. I mean, I don't live like *this*." I looked around her room and pulled her closer. "Why? You think I'm ghetto?"

"Not ghetto. Just maybe you've seen a few more things than I have."

I started rapping in her ear.

I'm a poor hoodlum
Wrong side of the tracks
Like a rich Russian breezy
Cuz she damn stacked.

She started laughing, and then there was a cough, and we ripped apart like somebody had sliced a knife between us. Irina's dad was standing in her doorway, staring at us. And if he could have shot me dead with one of those badass Russian machine guns, I guarantee he would have. He seemed even taller up close. I'm six foot two, and the dude was looking down.

"Irina, it's time for your friend to go home," he said. I was surprised that he didn't have an accent.

She was red. She grabbed the remote and turned off the music. "Okay," she said. "Um, Dad, this is Gabe."

"Nice to meet you, sir," I said.

His eyes went up and down me. I stood very straight. Damn, I was glad I was wearing new clothes. He didn't say anything, not a word. Finally he turned and walked away.

Irina looked like she wanted to evaporate.

"Hey, I wouldn't want me dancing with my daughter, either," I told her.

"Yeah, he's protective." There was an edgy sound in her voice. "Sorry he didn't say hi or anything."

I put away my phone and slung my backpack over my shoulder. "I think I won that round."

"No, that was incomplete. We only did one song each. Well, you did one and a half."

"Yeah, but you liked it so much, you danced to it."

"I was just being nice. You can't dance to Velvet Underground." Her words were teasing, but I could tell she was still upset about her dad. It *was* kind of rude, not even saying hi, like I was a total piece of junk. I wondered how she'd feel if she knew her mom was all up in my grill with the family and report card questions.

Irina walked me downstairs and out the door, and she waved as I walked down the driveway. I couldn't stop thinking about that moment when our bodies were touching. I should have kissed her.

CHAPTER SIX

When I got home from Irina's, all the lights were out except the TV, which was flickering in the living room, with loud rat-tat-tat-tats of gunfire.

Uh-oh. When my mom was depressed, she watched war movies. She said it put things in perspective. She always picked the gory ones, with close-ups of people getting their legs and faces blown off.

Sure enough, the DVD case for *Saving Private Ryan* was sitting on the coffee table. Mom was wearing the bathrobe she called "Old Ugly," sipping on something clear out of a jelly glass, and she looked to be near the bottom of a bag of potato chips. Mom cared a lot about her weight. She didn't touch chips unless things were *really* bad.

"Hey, Mom," I said.

"Hi, Gabe." Her voice sounded thick.

Crap. Bastard did something, I knew it. I went to sit next to her. "You okay?"

She nodded, eyes fixed on some dude dragging his thrashed body up a beach. She took a long swig of her drink. I knew how this would play out. She'd keep drinking until she was wasted, and then she'd cry on and off for the rest of the night, smoke enough packs to rot out at least one lung, and go through her photo albums, which would make her cry even harder. *Look how pretty I used to be,* she would say. Even worse, she didn't have anywhere to be tomorrow, so there was a good chance it would drag on into the next morning.

"Let's go to dinner," I said. "I want to take you out."

Mom's eyes flicked off the screen. "Oh, Gabe. You're sweet."

"I'm serious. We'll go somewhere nice."

She frowned, and I read her mind. "I have some money. I've been working."

"Really? Where?"

"Mowing lawns. People around here pay a lot." I was hoping she wouldn't realize grass didn't grow in Seattle this time of year.

Mom smiled so proudly that I felt horrible. "That's what you've been doing after school."

No, actually, I'd been kicking it with Kyle and Forrest and Matt, listening to music, and sometimes pretending to study when they did. Either that or texting back and forth with Irina.

I nodded. "Yeah. So let's go eat French food."

Mom thought anything French was classy. "Well . . ."

I picked up the remote and turned off the movie. "Mom!"

She put down her drink and gave me a watery smile. "Well, all right."

I jammed to my room to get some cash out of my closet and texted Kyle to ask about a good French place. He knew about that kind of thing. *Sans Souci,* he texted right back.

Mom met me downstairs rocking pre-Phil clothes—a puffy shirt and one of her tree-hugger skirts—which I was glad to see. I drove her car, because she wasn't too steady on her feet, and we were there in twenty minutes.

Mom cheered right up when she saw the place. "Hoh hoh fee fee," she whispered to me. It was small, with round tables and a lady singing in French on a stage. She was lipping the mic like it might kiss her back, but the music was pretty good.

The waiter looked at us like maybe we'd missed the turnoff for Mickey D's. "May I help you?"

Mom said back, just as snobby, "Table for two."

When we were seated, she spread her napkin in her lap and picked up the menu. "Oh no, Gabe. It's too expensive." But she was smiling. Mom loved to blow cash.

"Like that ever stopped you before."

"You're such a sweetheart. All right. But I'm getting the chicken Marseille." It was one of the cheaper things on the menu.

"Get something good!"

"No, I really want chicken Marseille."

I got the same thing, and we both had some bubbly water, because Mom said she didn't need any more alcohol. We shared a salad with cheese and pears.

Mom looked around at the paintings on the walls and the waiters in their suits. "This is beautiful. Thank you, Gabe."

"So, what did Phil do?" I asked.

Mom got a funny look. "'In the majority of cases, conscience is an elastic and very flexible article.' I found that today. It's Charles Dickens."

"He didn't tell his wife?" I guessed.

She nodded.

"Mom, you have to stop believing him when he says he'll do it. How many times has he said he would and then he didn't?"

"I know; I know. He just needs to get his courage up. He's staying with her out of guilt." Mom lowered her voice, playing with her fork. "They don't even sleep together. But she's so crazy, he's worried she'll hurt herself if he leaves."

I looked at my poor stupid mom. "You really believe he doesn't sleep with his wife?"

Mom's face got stiff. She picked up her sparkling water. "Yes, I do."

"Mom, Phil is a liar. He lies to his wife, so why wouldn't he lie to you?"

"Because we have a different relationship than they do!"

I should have stopped there, but I didn't. "Yeah, you do have a different relationship. She gets to live with him and use up his paychecks, and you just get to—" It was so bad I couldn't finish the sentence. "Mom, I can pay our rent. I'll work extra. You don't have to be with him." My brain was jumping ahead: How much would I have to sell to make rent? I'd have to expand to harder stuff, but that was okay.

"Gabe, thank you, but I want to be with him," said Mom.

I got mad. Because it was easier for me when I could think of her as the victim. But the truth, which she kept shoving in my face, was that it was completely 100 percent her own stupid fault.

"Fine." I pushed away my chicken, which I'd only taken a few bites of. Thirty-dollar chicken.

"Don't be mad, Gabe."

"I am mad. This whole thing is fucking stupid, and you keep doing it."

Mom set down her fork and took a deep breath. "You don't understand what love is."

I glared at her. "What you guys are doing isn't love."

She glared back. "I think I know when I love somebody."

"Well, he doesn't love you," I shot at her. "Love is an *action*, not a feeling." Where did I get that? I didn't know, but it stopped her in her tracks.

She closed her eyes for a second. Then she opened them and said, "Thank you, Gabe, for your teenage wisdom." She started sniffling.

"Aw, Mom, cut it out. Don't cry. I take it back. Phil's a gem. He's a freaking diamond, and he's going to marry you, and we'll all live happily ever after, okay?"

Mom brushed away her tears. "I'm sorry. I know I'm being an idiot. I know Phil is . . . I know what he is, okay?"

I watched her hopefully.

She took a tissue out of her purse. "He's everything I thought I never wanted in a guy. But I need to grow up, Gabe. You're almost out of high school. Don't you think it's time?" She gave me a shaky smile.

"Growing up means dating a toolbox? *Cheating* with him?"

She patted the tissue under her eyes. "That's the tough part. But you're not giving him credit for how responsible he is. He's providing for us in a way nobody ever has before. And he's smart." Mom idolized smart. It was her weak point.

"Smart, yeah, right," I said. "That guy is fuller of bull—"

"Enough." She cut me off. "He *is* smart. And I know you're right about some of the other things, but that doesn't change how I feel. Let's not talk about it anymore, okay?"

"Okay," I agreed. I actually did feel better, just hearing her say she knew I was right. If she wanted to go jumping off a roof, I couldn't stop her, but at least we both knew it was a hundred-foot drop.

She pushed my plate back toward me and said in a momish voice, "Eat."

I ate. My food wasn't worth thirty dollars, but I'd pay more than that to keep her from going on a bender. Mom was sober by the time we got home, and went to bed instead of getting into the photo albums.

♠ ♣ ♥ ♦

I'd been at Claremont High for a month, and it was pretty much killing me. We were on a quarter system, which I wasn't used to. The teachers actually kept track of who did their homework, corrected it, and threw pop quizzes at us all the time. So it didn't take them long to figure out I was stupid. I kept my head down and stayed pretty well under the radar, though.

Then a couple days after my mom's almost-bender, I was in English, the class I hated most, with Mueller, the teacher I hated most. She was straight Nazi, but wrapped in sugar, all blond hair and designer dresses. She was one of those teachers who can hear the smallest whisper and see through notes.

Mueller had just passed out copies of some play called *The Robbers*. It was written like two hundred years ago, so I knew it was bad. She was looking around the class, everybody trying not to meet her eyes so she wouldn't pick them.

She landed on me. "Gabe? You may take the role of Franz."

"No, thanks," I said.

A bunch of people laughed.

Mueller said, "Excuse me?"

I stared past her at the shiny Smart Board, where her writing was in perfect rows. "No, thanks."

Ms. Mueller rested her hand on her desk. "Would you care to explain yourself?"

I shook my head. Last time I read out loud was in fifth grade, and Mackenzie Carter started laughing and said I was stupid, so I had to kick her brother's ass. Most teachers, you tell them no a few times, they get the message and stop asking.

"And if I told you that you'll lose all your participation points for the day?"

I shrugged. People weren't giggling anymore; there was just this heavy, tense quiet. Forrest, in the seat next to me, gave me a weird look. My face was on fire. At my old school, this would have been no big deal, but here it was like, *Call the cops, a guy won't read out loud.*

"Gabriel, I'll give you one more chance to explain your failure to cooperate." Ms. Mueller's voice was very cold and she had a glint in her eyes. I realized she *liked* doing this.

Forrest suddenly cut in, kind of loud and obnoxious. "Schiller was more of a political revolutionary than an artist. Why do we even have to read him?"

Ms. Mueller's eyes jumped to him. "I'll answer that in a minute." She looked back at me.

"My dad says the teachers at this school are trying to politically indoctrinate us," Forrest said.

Ms. Mueller made a disgusted sound. "That's ridiculous."

He leaned forward in his seat. "Look, what was Schiller's agenda? His *real* political agenda? And what's so great about *The Robbers*, anyway? I mean, we don't have that much time in class. We could be reading Milton or Chaucer. Or if you really want Sturm und Drang, why aren't we reading Goethe?"

"You're wrong, Forrest!" snapped Ms. Mueller. "Schiller was nearly as influential as Goethe, and in my opinion, the better artist. And I don't know where you're getting your ideas about his politics. Read his biography. His work is a reaction against a personal experience in Karl Eugen's academy."

Forrest let air through his nose, as good as saying *bullshit*. "It was a lot more than that. I don't think we should be reading this. But I'll be Franz if you want."

Ms. Mueller looked from Forrest to me and back again. Forrest's dad had two buildings named after him—the new gym and the theater complex. But she couldn't let me off the hook completely. "Zero participation points today, Gabe. Forrest, you may be Franz. Eric, you may play Karl. The narrator I've divided into eight parts . . ."

I gave Forrest a look to let him know I appreciated it.

He grinned. He liked to mess with teachers. He knew more than most of them did, anyway. He didn't have to jump in like that, using his dad, though. I owed him.

After school that day, Matt asked me and Forrest and Kyle if we wanted to come over and watch the Broncos-Chargers game. Kyle was a Denver fan, and Matt was from San Diego, so it would be a nice tight match with some good yelling and trash talk.

We headed there straight from school. Matt had an awesome media room with a sick flat screen and recliners for everybody, although we all sat on the floor to be closer to the TV. His dad was obviously a sports freak, because there were signed jerseys on the wall and a glass case full of scorecards and a beat-up football signed by Walter Payton.

Matt's mom, this tiny Japanese lady, brought us a ton of food: sandwiches and cookies and bowls of rice crackers. The Broncos were destroying the Chargers, and it was funny to watch Matt, because whenever the Chargers took a hit, he had a personality change. His mouth did this thing, showing his teeth like he was going to bite someone, and he cussed and slapped the floor.

Of course we egged him on.

"Sorry about your team," Kyle said. "They're getting taken behind the woodshed."

Whump. Matt hit the floor. We all shook with laughter.

"Yeah, man," Kyle went on. "Look how their running back just coughed up the ball. Weak."

Whump.

Then Kyle showed his teeth and mumbled cusses and smacked the floor just like Matt, and we started cracking up. A commercial came on, which was probably a good thing, because Matt looked like he might kill someone. Kyle turned to me. "Did you already get the stuff for this weekend?" He was talking about when his parents went to Sonoma.

I shook my head. "I'm supposed to meet my guy on Wednesday."

"I got these Overlake friends. They want to know if you can hook them up, too."

Forrest glanced at him. "You talking about Jesse?"

"Yeah," said Kyle, "he's having a party at his lake house, and they want as much e as they can get."

Without a word, Matt got up and left the room.

We watched him disappear, and then Forrest said in a lower voice, "You know Olivia Gemelli? She was rolling at Morton's party, and she asked if she could get some more for her and those theater girls."

"I don't know." I glanced at the open door to the stairs. "I don't know any of those people." The thing with dope is, when you start dealing with strangers, it's only a matter of time before you get caught.

"They're cool," said Kyle. "I've known Jesse since we were four. If you want, I'll handle it."

"How much is he looking for?" I asked after a pause.

"He said as much as possible."

I thought about that. Tim would be happy. He'd texted me a couple times in the past week, wanting to know if I needed more. "What about Olivia?" I asked Forrest. "How much does she need?"

"She didn't say. You want me to ask her?"

I had a class with Olivia. She was cute and funny. "Yeah, that's cool. But don't say my name, okay?" I was doing math in my head. If this Jesse was for real, I could probably make a few grand, easy.

"That stuff was good. I've had a bunch of people ask about it." Kyle started ticking off a list of names. "Pete, that lacrosse dude,

Kelly Brian and his friends, Theresa Gaines, and that one skinny chick with the pink hair, what's her name? She has art with you."

"Huh," I said. "Let me talk to my friend, and I'll see."

A car commercial came on, showing a sweet Lexus. I couldn't afford a Lex unless I sold dope for like a year, but it did give me some ideas. I could get a decent used car for a lot less than a Lex. And it was time to lose the junk heap. It was getting embarrassing.

"I'm sure I can hook it up," I said more firmly.

"Cool," said Kyle. "I'll let Jesse know."

Then Matt was back with a six-pack of sodas under his arm, and the game came on again. Broncos were running the show.

My phone buzzed, and I checked the text. Irina.

?

We already had a text code. A question mark meant *What are you doing?*

I texted: *Watching fbl*

She came back: *What teams?*

Chargers v Broncos, I typed. I had a feeling I knew what was coming next.

Bet you lunch Chargers win.

I laughed out loud. Ever since I told her a contest was a bet, she'd been making bets about random things. She was a born competitor, and I had a plan for upping the stakes.

Kyle glanced at my phone. "Irina?"

I nodded and texted her: *You're on.*

Don't try to cheat. I'm checking the score.

"You're into that girl," said Kyle, watching me.

"She's good people."

Forrest looked at me then. "And she's a fine-ass *meeeeeeep*."

I smiled. "Well, yeah."

"I still can't believe you had the balls to get her number," said Kyle.

"Speaking of balls, you should have seen him in English." Forrest's eyes flicked back to the TV. "Ripping on Mueller."

I was hoping he'd leave that alone. "I just didn't feel like being Franz the Panzer Man," I said. "Whoa, check that pass."

But it didn't work. Kyle turned to me. "You screwed with Mueller? What'd you do?"

Forrest said, "She wanted him to read some play, and he was like, 'No, thanks.' Sounded like a CEO saying no to coffee."

Kyle cracked up. "Sweet!"

Matt was so busy watching the game, I'm not sure he even heard. But I could feel Forrest's eyes on me from the side. He was a smart guy, maybe the smartest guy I knew. He'd figure it out. I wondered if he'd decide he couldn't be friends with a loser.

I threw a rice cracker in the air and caught it with my mouth. Then Kyle had to do it, too, and pretty soon it turned into a contest. A cracker landed on the ground just as Matt's hand was coming down, and it got smashed, and we all lost it laughing. In the end, the Broncos won, and Forrest made up a song about the Chargers getting trampled like little girls in a bullfight. It was so twisted that even Matt had to laugh.

CHAPTER SEVEN

Just like I knew he would be, Tim was thrilled about the new customers. He met me at Red Robin himself instead of sending Missy. When I showed up, he was already in a booth, sucking on a Coke. He was a small dude with a scraggly goatee and eyes the light green of beach glass, and he was wearing the same ratty "Coors" T-shirt he always did.

He stood to give me a guy-hug, and I noticed he was moving kind of jerky. His arms were thinner than I remembered, and seriously cut. "Ordered you a shake." He nodded at a drink on the table. "You always used to get those, huh?"

I smiled. Back when they were first dating, his dad and my mom would give us kids twenty bucks to get out of the house and camp in Mickey D's for a couple hours. "Yeah, and you got the McMuffins. Those were nasty."

Tim nodded. "Oh yeah. I don't like those anymore. So how you been, man? How you like it up there?"

"Can't complain. I made some friends." I was about to tell him about Kyle and Forrest and Matt, but I saw his eyes darting and I realized he wasn't really interested.

"That's good; that's good." Tim lowered his voice. "I've got what we talked about, and I put in some extra. We don't want to have to be doing these runs all the time, so I just thought I'd pad you a little. Seems like you got good demand over there. We can settle accounts at the end of the month."

I frowned. "Naw, I don't want to be having a bunch extra. That's how people get busted."

"It's not much. Come on. It's a pain in the ass to drive all the way out here."

"Yeah, but what if I don't get rid of it?"

"You will. Look how fast you been moving product."

I drew on my shake. He had a point. I knew I could get rid of it if I wanted to. And the cash was official. I'd already got some new threads and kicks.

"There's a backpack under the table," Tim said. "After I leave, stick around and finish your drink, then take it with you. Cool?"

"Cool." I wished he would slow down, ask how I was really doing, act like we'd actually lived together for a few months instead of making this straight business. But Tim was older than me, and I guess he just thought of me as his sister's friend.

♠ ♣ ♥ ♦

That Friday in visual arts, one of the office runners brought me a slip calling me to the counselor's office. I'd been half-asleep, thinking about Irina, but when Mrs. McVeigh dropped the thing on my desk, I jerked up. I'd unloaded a bunch of Tim's backpack the day before, and I looked at the candy-pink paper and thought about running for the parking lot.

"You okay, Gabe?" Mrs. McVeigh gave me a strange look.

I nodded, stuffed my book in my backpack, and headed out. I was mentally scanning my locker, my pockets, my car. Clean, clean, and clean. I knew better than to bring anything to school. But what if somebody had narced?

I half turned toward the lot, then turned back around and kept going. I'd watched enough movies to know I had to play it cool. Still, as I opened the door to Ms. Tacquard's office, my heart was hammering like it wanted out of my chest. She was one of those people who took her job too seriously. And she was a bulldog about dope; I'd heard there was a one-strike policy.

"Hi, Gabe," Ms. T. said as I walked in. "Have a seat." She was a tall, gray-haired lady, and she never wore any jewelry or makeup. She was in her big leather chair, which she'd pulled to the side of her scarily clean desk. That pull-to-the-side trick was supposed to make me feel like I could trust her. They all did it. I sat down and looked at her framed diplomas on the wall. There were about five of them.

"Gabe, I was wondering if we could chat about how you're doing with the transition to Claremont." Ms. Tacquard leaned back in her chair. She looked like a wooden toy trying to relax. "More specifically, how are you doing academically?"

Relief made me actually smile. "Fine. Doing good."

"That's not what your teachers are saying." She glanced at a folder on the desk.

I'd played this game plenty of times. I tried to look sorry, although I was so glad it wasn't about drugs that it probably came off like a smirk. "Sorry, Ms. Tacquard. I'll try harder."

Her eyelids lowered a notch, and I could see her going into "tough" mode. "I'm afraid we need to be more proactive than that." She opened the folder and started flipping through papers. "This is the test you failed in biology last week. This is the English paper you turned in a week late, and which received a grade of D. This is your math practice final, which you failed." She set the folder back on her desk. "Gabriel, I need to impress upon you the importance of these grades."

Her strategy worked. F-D-F was a bad lineup, even for me. Not that I'd admit it to anybody, but I'd been trying. Those damn tests. Every time I got one back, I *knew* I'd had the right answer, but I'd filled in the wrong bubble for some reason. Bubble tests had screwed with me my whole life. But I wasn't giving Tacquard the satisfaction of seeing that she rattled me.

"Okay, Ms. T. I know they're important."

She sighed. "You're close to failing three of your classes. The quarter ends in three weeks. If you don't pick up your grades, you'll have to repeat them to graduate. And that's not going to help your chances of getting into a good college."

"I'm not going to college," I said.

It was like I threw a rock through the window. She stared at me. She cleared her throat. "Gabe, that's a pretty big statement. Do you want to talk about it?"

I looked away. "Nothing to talk about. I'm just not college material." I couldn't read for longer than ten minutes without getting dizzy. I couldn't write worth crap. And I couldn't stand the thought of another four years locked in a white-walled cage with adults pouring bullshit through a tube into my ears.

There was a long silence. Ms. Tacquard stared at me with narrowed eyes. "Well, I hope you'll reconsider. A college degree can open a lot of doors. In the meantime, we have an after-school tutoring program that I think would benefit you. We offer sessions on Monday, Wednesday, and Friday afternoons. Would you like me to sign you up?"

"No, that's okay."

Ms. T. let out a quiet *hmsh* through her nose. "All right, Gabe. You understand that I'll be speaking with your mother about this. It's a school policy to keep parents informed."

I didn't answer. Mom wasn't going to take the news easy. She'd been getting her hopes up, asking where I was going to apply, and even throwing out "Florida State," which she loved because she once dated a guy who played football there.

I stood up and slung my backpack over my shoulder.

Ms. T. said in a gentler voice, "Don't give up on yourself, Gabe. Those analytical scores on your ninth-grade battery were good. With tutoring, I know you can pull up your grades."

I looked at the door, waiting for her to let me go.

"And please, think a little more about college."

I felt my neck getting hot. Why should I think about college? Everybody acted like it gave you a passport into the Real Person Club, instead of an expensive-ass brainwashing.

"Gabe?"

I walked out before she had a chance to say anything else.

When Kyle stopped to get books before study hall, I was waiting at his locker. "Hey, man," he said, sounding surprised.

"Did your parents already leave for Sonoma?" I asked.

"Yeah, this morning."

"Let's bail and start the party early. I can't handle math right now."

He grinned and started dialing his lock. "Done."

A few minutes later, I was tailing Kyle's Jeep down the I-405. We hit Bartell's first. He wasn't messing around; he filled up a cart with candy, Vicks, a pack of binkies, orange juice, sherbet, glow sticks, a musical top with flashing lights, light-up Hacky Sacks, and Christmas lights.

After paying for everything, Kyle kicked me half a G for the e and Oxies. I felt a little bad about making such a big profit. But if I gave him a discount this time, he'd wonder why I hadn't done it before, and it would be confusing. It was his parents' money, anyway.

Then we headed to his place to set up. Kyle lived in a modern house that looked like somebody took a giant cement box, cut windows in it, and dropped it in the middle of the White House lawn. There were some ugly Lego-looking bushes and a jelly bean–shaped pool, but the inside was dope. The staircase looked like it was floating, and the carpet was made out of thick white stuff like grass from another planet.

Kyle got busy picking out tracks and setting up a candy buffet. The colors had to be in order from light to dark: Lemonheads all the way to Junior Mints. Kyle was like that. He seemed chill, but he was actually a freak about organization.

I sipped a beer and mostly let him do it. I was feeling kind of messed up about the talk with Ms. T. *College.* That word was eating through my brain.

Ms. T. had looked so shocked when I said I wasn't going. I'd known for a while, and I was fine with it. But being around all these trust-fund kids was messing with me. You could just tell they would stick their head in an oven if they didn't get into college— and not just any old college, but Stanford or something.

FDF. *Fucking Dimwit Fool.* I looked at Mr. 4.0 Rower, setting out a drug buffet, and I wanted to know how he did it. How did he stay focused? Remember what he read? Fill in the right bubbles? Were there tricks?

But it wasn't the kind of thing you could ask.

I drank my beer fast and opened another. Kyle put on some tunes, and pretty soon the girls arrived in a pack—Erin and Becky and three others, who were mad fine but off-limits because Becky had staked me out. Girls have secret laws like that, and it screws things up for us guys pretty good.

We all took our pills right away and just hung around, waiting for them to kick in. Everybody except Matt. Dude was straighter than a ruler. I knew he'd leave in a little while; he didn't like being around trashed people.

Kyle went into Host Boy mode, handing out candy and party favors. Forrest and Matt got into some argument about MIDI, and what would have happened if somebody had invented a different computer language for music first. This girl Samantha was practically sitting on Forrest's lap, and another girl, Melanie, was leaning against Matt, but they might as well have been pillows with boobs and hair for all the attention Matt and Forrest paid them.

Becky was getting pretty friendly, too. You could tell she was starting to roll. She kept running her fingers through her hair, and then petting the carpet like it was a cat, and smiling at me. I wasn't feeling anything myself, only a little buzzed from the beer.

E wasn't my drug. I didn't like that fake-happy feeling, acting as if I loved the whole world—because I didn't. I only loved a few people. Even when I was rolling, there was a little voice whispering, *This is bullshit. You don't feel this way. It's just the drug.*

Crank was another story. I felt like myself on crank, only better. But that scared me, because they say feeling that way is the surest sign a drug can hook you. Besides, I'd seen what the stuff did to Tim's friend Julio, who was tweaking so hard, he ripped the skin off his face because he thought there were bugs crawling underneath. Missy and me were there—it was sixth grade—and we couldn't stop him. Tim wouldn't let us call 9-1-1 because he didn't want Julio getting arrested, but Julio said we should have. He had nasty scars after that.

Becky scooted closer to me and laid her head in my lap. "Tickle my hair."

I started running my fingers on her scalp, and she made little moaning noises, which made me and Kyle look at each other and crack up. He gave me a look, like, *All yours*, but I wasn't feeling it yet.

Then a good song came on, with a phat beat, and I started to feel waves of sensation. But I was so weird, I kept fighting them.

Feels so good right now—

Bullshit.

All these cool people, your friends—

Won't remember you once they're in college.

Nice girl, take her in a bedroom and—

Wish it was Irina.

Chill out, you bastard, and have fun—

I'm a loser. I don't belong here.

Finally I got so sick of my own stupid brain that I stopped tickling Becky's hair and leaned down and whispered, "I heard there's a concert in one of these bedrooms. We should go check it out." She giggled and stood up and took my hand, and we went upstairs, found a good room, and shut the door.

CHAPTER EIGHT

Saturday morning, I woke up lying on carpet as thick as a mattress, under a giant wood shelf with mirrors. There were rows of shiny circles hanging over my head like spotlights, and it took me a second to realize they were upside-down glasses. I rolled over and knocked into . . . an empty bottle of maraschino cherries.

The cherries triggered my memory. When Becky and I had come back downstairs the night before, everybody was acting like idiot candy ravers, sucking on lollipops and listening to trance music that sounded like somebody's three-year-old got hold of a synthesizer. I wanted to get away from Becky, who kept stroking my hand, so I went bar hunting and got into some wack scotch that tasted like motor oil. Then I got hungry, so I started eating the cherries.

After that . . . I didn't remember.

I scraped myself off the floor and stumbled to the living room, where some of the others were passed out. Binkies and candy wrappers and Christmas lights were everywhere, like baby elves had a party. Kyle was snoring, lollipop-colored spit trickling out of his mouth onto the white couch. The girls were lying in a heap like puppies. I tiptoed so I wouldn't wake anybody up.

"Hey," said a weird voice.

I almost jumped out of my skin.

It was Forrest. He was wrapped in a blanket and leaning against the sliding glass door. He'd been sitting so still, I hadn't realized he was there. His eyes were vampire red and he was holding an Orange Crush.

"Hey," I said. "You have fun last night?"

"I'm still having fun." He pulled his other hand from under the blanket and shook a pill bottle at me. It was the Oxies.

I frowned. "How many did you do?"

"Five or six. I don't know. This shit is awesome. Can you get me more?" There was a hungry look on his face.

A surge of warning jumped into my chest. "That might be hard to hook up," I lied. I knew tweakers; I knew junkies; I knew addicts; and suddenly I could tell that Forrest had that in him.

He shrugged. "That's cool. I'll find it somewhere else."

"Okay, man. See you." I walked out the front door. The sunlight felt like it was cutting me open. I got into my car and had to sit a couple minutes so I wouldn't heave whatever was left of that nasty scotch. I pictured Forrest lying dead on the pavement after an OD. Living under the bridge. Screwing men for drugs. It would be my fault because I got him started.

No, wait. He was rich. Okay, he'd be in rehab in some dope spa with Hollywood hotties and fresh carrot juice and massage.

Still not that cool.

I felt like hitting the steering wheel. I was being paranoid. Forrest wasn't doing anything I hadn't done myself, so I needed to stop acting like his grandma. And Becky would understand that we just hooked up because we were rolling, and not because I liked her or anything. Right?

And college could go to hell.

I needed aspirin. Something. I hit the gas and peeled out.

♠ ♣ ♥ ♦

Guess who was there when I got home? I walked inside, and as I headed up the stairs, I heard giggling, footsteps, and the bathroom door slamming shut. My favorite man in the world was at the kitchen table, chowing down on eggs and bacon.

"Um, Phil?" my mom said through the bathroom door.

"Hi, Gabriel." Phil took a sip of orange juice, looking pleased with himself.

"Phil?" my mom said again.

He glanced at the closed door. "Yes, honey?"

I stood there. I had a quick fantasy of walking over and slamming his face into his plate.

"Could you bring me . . . something from my closet?" said my mom.

Phil stood and headed upstairs to the bedroom.

I ran myself a glass of water and drank it fast. I had that good warmed-up feeling I get before a fight. I made a fist, imagined crashing it into Phil's meaty face. I walked to the other side of the table, in the narrow part of the kitchen where it opened into the living room. He'd have to walk past me when he came back down.

There were steps, and Phil turned the corner of the stairs. He was holding my mom's clothes. The ready-to-blast feeling drained out of me like sand. If I hit him, my mom would come running out naked, and . . . I couldn't do it.

"Smells like you've had quite a night," said Phil as he passed me, Mom's dress dangling off his finger like a prize.

"Fuck you." I stalked up to my room.

I lay on my bed and stared at the ceiling. Life was messed up to the googol degree (I had learned what a googol was the other day in math). I was trapped. I would never be one of the smart, rich ones. I would always be the piece of shit getting stepped on. I couldn't even protect my own mom. I probably wouldn't graduate high school.

And if I did, what would I do then? Keep dealing and do a bid and get turned into some gang member's bitch because I was a pretty boy? Work roofing or construction and jack up my body by the time I was thirty, then get screwed out of workman's comp like they all do? Before I moved to Redmond, those things seemed like normal possibilities. Now they felt like low-life bullshit for suckers.

Screw feeling depressed, I decided, and tried to think of something good. I had a fat honey roll in my pocket; that was good. I was going over to Irina's to watch a movie later; that was good. I pictured her resting her head on my shoulder, cuddling on that big white couch and talking. When I was with her, I didn't stress about anything (except maybe her dad).

I checked the clock. It was way too long until I could go to her house. And Phil was like a two-hundred-pound turd in my living room, sending waves of stink right through the ceiling. But I felt too torn up to leave.

I looked around my room and saw my schoolbooks staring at me from my dresser. Kyle and Matt and Forrest spent hours every day hitting their books. It was the first time I'd had friends who actually studied.

I made myself get out of bed and pick up my science book. I used to be okay at science. I even liked it, especially the stuff about human bodies. Maybe that was why I'd lied and told Irina I wanted to be a doctor. In a magical world where I could focus, it might be true.

I opened my bio textbook to chapter four. I had a test in microbiology on Wednesday. Mr. Newport said it was 15 percent of our grade.

Bolded words jumped at me like thugs: Taq polymerase. Thermostable. Protein denaturing. Cloning vector. Plasmid. I lay back down and tried to read for a second, but the letters kept getting smaller and sliding off the page. It was like aliens talking. *Greetings to your queen.*

I closed the book. I wasn't made for this. I should drop out.

I felt relieved just thinking about it. But Mom would die. And I only had a year left . . .

Maybe I could transfer back to Jefferson, where you could swing Cs if you could write your own name. I knew Mom wasn't about moving, but what if I crashed with one of my boys in White Center, just on weeknights?

I started mentally scrolling through the choices: Jerrod's parents fought too much; Andy's mom was a head case who saved everything, so you had to walk around stacks of magazines to get through their house; but Mike's dad would let me crash with them. They had that space heater in the garage. I got excited for about a minute, and then I started thinking about having no place to bring girls, no hot food, no furniture. Plus, Mike had three little brothers, and they lived on government cheese and weight-gain shakes. It would be wrong to step on their food or their space.

My brain crawled in circles. Live in a shed so I could finish high school so I could get a piece of paper that said I wasn't a complete dumbass so I could work a job that I hated so I could come home to my sad digs so I could wake up the next morning and do it over again.

High school wasn't worth it. I'd stay at Claremont, and if they wanted to flunk me, let them.

Once I decided that, I felt better. I chucked the book off the bed, set my alarm, and went to sleep until it was time to go to Irina's.

♠ ♣ ♥ ♦

I got to Irina's house at seven, because I slept through my alarm. She was mad, even though I was only an hour late.

"I was just getting ready to leave," she said when she answered the door. She was all dressed, with shoes on and everything. I was relieved to see her mom wasn't behind her.

"I'm sorry. I was sleeping, and I didn't hear my alarm."

She rolled her eyes. "You were sleeping at six p.m."

"Yeah," I said. I wasn't in the mood to beg. "I went out late last night. Come on. You're not even going to let me in?"

She sighed but stepped aside.

I hung up my coat on the coat tree and caught her watching me. "I knew you liked me," I said.

She huffed. "What are you talking about?"

I looked into her pretty brown eyes and took a step toward her. "Friends can be late and it doesn't matter." She backed up, and I took another step. "It's okay. Just admit it."

She pushed my chest. "Gabe, cut it out! You're so conceited!" But she was grinning.

I didn't let her move me. There was about an inch between us. "Admit it."

"I do not like you."

I put my hands on her waist and leaned down and whispered in her ear, "Well, I wish you would." I could smell her sweet, clean shampoo and see the corner of her mouth trying not to smile. Then I straightened and said, "You gonna show me this subtitle thing or not?"

"If you mean one of the greatest films ever made, yes."

"Do you have anything to eat while we watch?" I had that hollow, thrashed feeling you get after a night of too much partying and not enough food.

"Sure. Come on." Irina led the way to the kitchen, which was so big you could have stuck a couch in it and called it a living room. Everything was wood and tile, and there were pots hanging from the ceiling and paintings on the wall. Who hangs paintings in the kitchen?

Irina pulled stuff from the fridge and cabinets: white ball-shaped cookies, and cookies that looked like squashed donuts, and Cokes, and a chunk of grayish stuff that I was worried might be cheese. Also a box with foreign writing on it—some kind of Russian food.

"So how did your recital go?" I asked while she was getting out plates. She'd told me the week before that she had a big-deal recital on Friday night.

She opened the box. "Terrible."

"What happened?" I tried to see her face, but her hair was hanging like a curtain.

She started setting thin white crackers on a plate. "I didn't practice enough, and I didn't play as well as I should have."

I frowned. "You practice six hours a day. How much more could you do?"

"More. But I'm tired, and I didn't." Irina closed the box and turned to face me. The bright kitchen lights made her look extra pale.

"Of course you're tired. You work too hard. I mean, seriously, how could you practice more than six hours a day?"

She shrugged. "Other professionals work eight or ten hours a day at their jobs. It's no different, really."

"Okay, but you're not a professional. You're seventeen. And anyway, normal people spend like half their work time texting, getting coffee, or whatever. You're alone in some room with your violin."

She opened one of the Cokes and took a drink. It was regular, not diet like most girls drank. "Yeah, I know," she said. "I'm getting kind of sick of it." Her voice had an edge.

I was about to tell her to chuck the stupid thing, but Mom says sometimes girls don't want advice; they just want to talk. So I said, "Uh-huh."

She fiddled with the pop-top. "I'm worried that . . . I have this feeling I'm going to be, like, thirty? And I'll look back and think I never got to be a teenager."

"That sucks," I said.

"Yeah. And I don't even know if it's worth it." She was staring at me, eyes big, and I could tell she'd thought a lot about this. "Do you know how many prodigies just fail when they get to be adults? It's called the Icarus effect. You fly too high, and your wings melt."

I opened my mouth to remind her she wasn't a prodigy, and then I realized maybe it wasn't the time. "You should take a break," I said instead.

She leaned against the counter next to me. "My parents would freak. They've been building me toward this my whole life, and if I mess it up, it'll be like I totally failed them."

"That's harsh. Sorry they're like that."

Irina frowned. I should have known better than to say that. People can complain like crazy about their own parents, but if you agree with them, it's a slap.

"They love me," she said, kind of sharp. "That's why they're pushing me. Americans don't understand that. They think loving kids means being easy on them."

I felt annoyed, because I was getting tired of the *Americans* comments, and yeah, my mom had always been easy on me, and here I was, a total screwup, and there Irina was, a genius. But my mom loved me. I never had to wonder about that for a second.

Irina must have seen something on my face, because she added quickly, "There're a lot of different ways of loving kids, that's all I'm saying. I just don't want you to think my parents are horrible."

"I don't think that."

"I just . . . I need a break. I feel tight in here." She touched her chest. "And I know it's hurting my music."

"Have your parents send you to Hawaii," I told her. "That's like, what, one day's salary for your dad?"

"Yeah, a vacation would be nice," she said. "Except it wouldn't really be a vacation if they were there."

I picked up her hand and started playing with it. "*I'll* take you on vacation. We'll go to Vegas and lie by the hotel pool. I'll teach you to play poker." I was only half kidding. Vegas had always been my vacation fantasy. I'd seen the ads; those dudes always looked like they were having the times of their lives. And they were doing stuff I was good at: drinking, playing cards.

Irina didn't take her hand away. "That sounds fun."

I pulled her into a hug. "It would be fun. We'd get all dressed up and check out the Strip and the casinos. And we'd go see that one circus. You know the commercial with the trapeze guys?"

She let her head rest on my chest. "Cirque du Soleil." She was tiny, and she smelled good. It felt amazing to have her in my arms. I wanted so badly to kiss her, but I could tell I had to take it slow or she might run away.

"Yeah, them," I said softly. "Then we'd go out to the clubs. I want to dance with you."

"Except we're both seventeen, so I guess we couldn't do any of that stuff, except maybe walk down the Strip," she said a little sadly.

"I have an ID," I told her. "I could get you one if you want."

"Are you serious?" Irina pulled back and looked at my face. When she saw I was for real, she gave a delighted giggle. "Okay, get me one, then."

"I'll set it up."

Irina looked excited, and it was the best feeling in the world knowing I'd made her feel better. Then she asked, "How do you keep everything in balance? Like, Claremont is supposed to be intense, and I'm sure you have good grades if you're going to medical school, but you know how to have fun, too. Sometimes I feel like I forgot how to have fun."

It was like somebody vacuumed the good feeling out of my chest. But I kept smiling. "It's not that hard. I just study."

"That's cool." She pulled out of my arms and gave me a mischievous look. "Gabe, let's not watch the movie. Teach me how to play poker."

I grinned at her. "Done."

♠ ♣ ♥ ♦

We took our food to the "game room" instead of the "movie room." It was off the hook. There were two big brown leather couches, a pool table, a giant flat screen, and a wall of shelves filled with games. And you guessed it: more paintings. They were all of fruit, wine, and dead birds lying around on tables like somebody just happened to drop them there. I didn't see the appeal.

It took Irina about a minute to learn Texas Hold'em, and she wasn't too bad. I let her win twice, and she started bragging so hard that I didn't have the heart to tell her I was going easy on her. I looked at her sitting across from me on the carpet, blond hair falling in her eyes, face stretching from smiling so much, and I knew she was having fun. Even if I was useless in every other way, I was good at this one thing.

"Gabe," Irina said, dealing the cards like I showed her, "prepare to lose again."

"Okay. But if I win, I get a prize."

"What?"

"You know."

She blushed. But she said calmly, "Well, you won't win."

I beat her extremely fast.

When I showed her my hand, she ducked her head and her cheeks got red like somebody was turning up the color. I laughed and swept the cards out of the way. She glanced up at me. I leaned closer and looked into her eyes, at the excitement and shyness and smartness and humor shining out of them. And I finally kissed her. It was . . . too hot to explain. We matched each other so good, and I knew she'd been wanting me as bad as I'd been wanting her.

CHAPTER NINE

That night when I got home, I ran upstairs feeling like I was in sixth grade again and just had my first kiss with Shana Meyers. Except this was better. The house was quiet, and it had a no-Phil feeling. As I rounded the landing, I noticed a crack of light under my door. Had I left my light on?

I pushed open the door, and Mom raised her head from my desk. She'd been resting her head on her arms. She gave me a fuzzy smile. "Hi, baby. What time is it?"

"I don't know, like eleven. What are you doing in here?"

Mom sat up and blinked. "Um . . . oh, I just wanted to talk to you."

I sighed and dropped on my bed, the good feeling leaking out of me. I knew what this was about.

"Your counselor called," Mom said quietly.

We looked at each other. We'd been playing this game a long time, and Mom understood. She was stupid in the same way I was.

"I know you're trying, honey."

"Yeah."

"But she's worried. She said you're failing three classes."

"Yeah."

Mom put a hand over her eyes as if she could rub away her thoughts. "Gabe, we moved here so—"

"No, we didn't." I cut her off. "Let's not go there."

"Well, then you have to tell me what's going on." She sounded upset. "The worst grade you ever got before was a C minus! Claremont is supposed to be so good!"

"Good means *hard!*" I stood up and went to the closet, hoping she'd take the hint and leave.

Mom was quiet for a second. "Ms. Tacquard mentioned tutoring."

"I'm not doing that." I pawed through my laundry for a clean T-shirt.

"Hold on," she said, and left the room. I changed quickly and sat down at my desk. I would have paid a lot to fast-forward through whatever was coming.

In a few minutes, Mom was back with her angel book. She stood in the doorway and flipped through until she found the right page. "'The roots of education are bitter, but the fruit is sweet.' Aristotle." She gave me a hopeful look that almost made me want to laugh.

"Mom, quotes don't fix everything."

"No, but sometimes they put things in perspective. Couldn't you bring them up to Cs?"

I shrugged. "I'll try."

"Okay, but if it doesn't work, you're doing the tutoring program." Mom was digging deep, trying to pull up some authority.

"No," I said. We almost never faced off like this. I tried to soften it. "I'll bring up the grades, okay?"

"Okay, honey," Mom said, but she sounded defeated. She went to hug me, then turned instead, as if she'd meant to pull down the window shade. She was a very huggy person normally, but she knew I didn't like to be comforted about being stupid. Because she didn't, either.

♠ ♣ ♥ ♦

On Monday, I did something I'd never done before in my life. It actually made me feel a little sick, because I was basically admitting I couldn't handle my business. I told Newport, my science teacher, that I needed help.

Partly I did it for my mom, because it was the only way I could think of to bring up my grades without tutoring. But mostly I did it because of Irina. She was what I wanted, maybe in a for-real way, and I was finally getting somewhere with her. But if she knew I wasn't graduating, and that all the stuff about me being a doctor was lies, she would run. And she'd be right. Because she was going somewhere in life, and she deserved a guy who was dialed in, too.

Also, science had always been the subject I could count on, and I wasn't going to fail it. I just wasn't.

So I went to see Newport after school. He was my favorite teacher at Claremont, hands down. He always looked like he was half-asleep, except when he got excited about some science idea.

He had a cute wife, and on his desk he had a picture of her holding a chubby little kid that looked just like him. You could tell he was crazy about both of them, because he was always mentioning little stories that had to do with his family and saying "my wife" this and "my son" that. It was nice.

"Of course I'll help, Gabe," he said when I asked. "Let's set up a study schedule. How many afternoons a week can you swing?"

I hadn't thought about giving up time after school. "How about lunch?"

"I have to eat, buddy." Newport patted his big stomach.

"Can we do it every other week?"

"If you're serious about getting caught up, I don't think that's going to cut it. How about twice a week for an hour? Monday and Wednesday?"

"Okay," I said, not too happily.

Newport wanted to shake on it, which I did, although it was cheesy. He looked me in the eyes and said, "We'll get you back on track, Gabe. Count on it." It was obvious he was just dying to pull me out of whatever trash can I lived in and dust me off and give me a future. The problem with Claremont High was they didn't have enough losers, so when one came along, they got excited about it.

I got out of there and headed to the parking lot. I couldn't believe I'd just signed away two afternoons a week. But I knew Newport was right; it would take at least that much to pull up my grade. Now I needed a strategy to handle English and Algebra II.

For English, I'd just buy a term paper online. I'd done that before with tough teachers. When I wrote my own stuff, papers would come back bleeding, and my teachers would get all annoyed and say I needed to proofread. The thing they didn't know was I'd read the damn papers like ten times before I turned them in, and I never saw any of the mistakes.

Anyway, there was a Costco of papers online, and that would fix my problem. But I needed to pass math to graduate. As long as there wasn't a bubble test, I thought I could probably pull it off.

Somebody called my name, and at first I barely noticed, I was so caught up thinking about school. But then I heard it again and turned around. It was Becky. She cut through the parking lot and hugged me hello. She was all North Faced out, with her long brown hair tucked under a pink ski cap, looking like the girl your mom is dying for you to take to prom.

Shoot. She'd texted me the day before, and I sort of hadn't texted back.

"What's up?" I said.

"I don't know," she said, smiling up at me. "What's up with you?"

"Nothing."

She hitched her bag higher on her shoulder. "What are you doing right now?"

"I have to study." It was an excuse, but looking at Becky, it gave me an idea. "I just found out I'm failing a bunch of classes."

Becky's eyes got wide. "Seriously?"

"Yeah, I'm pretty stupid," I said.

"Gabe, don't say that about yourself."

"No, I am. I'll probably drop out."

Becky looked horrified, and then she hugged me again, and I realized too late she might be one of those girls who like to "save" guys. "I'll help you study!" she said.

"No, that's okay," I said quickly. "I actually think I want to drop out."

She looked confused. "But you said you were going to study."

I looked at the cars streaming out of the lot. "Well, I haven't totally decided yet."

"Gabe." Becky slipped her hands around me and rubbed my back. "Don't stress about this. You're not going to drop out. One thing I know is academics. I'll help you, okay? This school is kind of intense, but you can totally handle it."

I looked down at her. She was rubbing too soft; not enough pressure. "Thanks, Becky. That's sweet."

Her blue eyes were big, and I could smell her vanilla lotion. "Seriously, I tutor my neighbor, Isabel. She's a junior. I'm helping her get ready for the SAT."

"Okay." I pulled away gently.

"Do you want me to help right now? I could come over."

For half a second I thought about having her come over—not to study, obviously—but then I decided no. Becky was already too into me. It would be messed up to lead her on. And I had to keep my eyes on the prize, a certain freaky homeschooled Russian with an attitude.

"Nah, but thanks. That's really cool of you." I smiled at her. I learned a long time ago never to explain much to women. That way they can't argue with you.

"Okay, well, if you change your mind . . ." She touched my arm again.

"Thanks, Becky." I thought about kissing her on the top of the head, to let her know she was sweet, but then I thought she might get the wrong idea. "Later."

♠ ♣ ♥ ♦

I got in my car and headed out of the lot. Had I really just turned down a nice, hot girl who wanted me? Irina was doing things to my head. I turned toward the I-5, because I had to make a run to White Center. Tim said no more deals in public.

I'd hooked up Kyle's friends, and Olivia and the drama girls had wanted more than I expected, so I was already out of product. The cash had been building in my closet, fat rolls shoved in old sneakers and the pockets of shirts I never wore, and I was getting close to a car. I could probably buy one already, just not brand-new. A sweet Altima had been on Craigslist for almost a week. I was worried it might disappear, but I had to time my offer just right and let the sellers build up some anxiety.

Halfway to the on-ramp, I had an idea about doing two errands at once. Then I had second thoughts. Then I decided I was done being weak. I called Irina. "You want to get that ID?" I asked when she answered.

"Are you serious?"

I loved how surprised she sounded. "Yeah, I'll pick you up. But my car is a complete piece of junk, so you can't say anything about it."

There was a pause. "What are you talking about? We went to the party, remember? Your car is fine."

"That was a rental."

There was a silence while it sank in. I wasn't too worried. I'd figured out a few things about Irina. She wasn't one of those puffed-up divas who would scream at an off-brand shirt. My ride would make her laugh, and that was what she needed. Besides, I was tired of fronting. Of course, I was still fronting in other ways, like about my future, but she *would* care about that.

Finally she said, "I can't believe you rented a car to impress me."

"I knew when I saw you I wanted to be with you." I was already pulling a U-turn.

There was another silence, a good one, I thought. Then she said, "How come you decided to show me your real car now?"

"Because it's funny. And I'm getting a new car soon, anyway, so you don't have to worry about me driving you around in this thing for long."

Irina gave a delighted giggle. "Okay, pick me up. What should I wear?"

"Something dark. Something that makes you look older."

"I can't believe we're doing this," she said.

"I'll be there in ten minutes."

♠ ♣ ♥ ♦

Irina laughed her head off when she saw my ride. She climbed into her seat, chuckling, and then she really lost it, pounding her knee with her breath coming in gasps.

"I told you," I said.

"It's epic," she wheezed. She pointed at a white sticker on the glove box: "There are two types of pedestrians, quick and dead."

"It was that way when I got it. It won't come off." I pulled her in for a kiss. She stopped laughing and kissed me back, good and hard, and held the back of my neck as if she was hungry for more.

"Damn, Irina," I said when she let go. "You trying to make me lose it right here in front of your house?"

She smiled proudly. Whoever said good girls are the freakiest was dead-on.

I pulled out of her driveway, and she dug in her bag. "I brought some music, but I don't know, does this thing even have a sound system?"

"Very funny." Actually, it had an excellent sound system. I'd made sure of that. I turned it on to show her.

She frowned. "The bass is way out of balance. Here." She fiddled with the knobs and slid in one of her CDs. "You don't want the bass to overwhelm everything else; otherwise you lose texture."

"Speak for yourself." I paused. "Irina, what *is* this?"

"Timati," she said. "It's Russian rap."

And it was. If you had told me Russians were trying to rap, I would have died laughing. But this dude had solid beat, he had power, and even in Russian, I could tell he had rhyme. I pictured a big fur-wearing, squinty-eyed mutha with one of those bear hats.

"He's good, isn't he?" Irina said knowingly.

"Yeah," I admitted. "Although I never would have thought Russians could rap."

Irina gave me a triumphant look. I reached for her hand and held it while I drove. Her thumb tapped softly inside my palm.

CHAPTER TEN

When we got past the 509, I hit Roxbury Street and drove into White Center. Roxbury is a straight shot, and with every block the houses get a little older, and the cars get a little more thrashed, and pretty soon you start noticing every other store is a liquor store, and then you see bars on the windows, and then you realize, oh crap, when did everybody turn into gangsters? And then you're in White Center.

Irina was staring out the window in fascination. "This is your old neighborhood?"

"Yeah. We lived here six years. But New York always felt like home."

"Everybody from New York says that, even the Russians."

"Well, it *is* the best place in the world." I swung down Twenty-Sixth and pulled up outside Missy's beat-up old ranch house, which had a rusty pickup permanently parked on the lawn. "Wait here, I gotta do something really fast."

Irina frowned. "What do you have to do?"

I hadn't thought this part out very well, I realized. "Just drop off something for my friend."

"Can I come with you?"

"I'll only be a second. Don't worry, this hood is totally safe during the day."

Irina looked annoyed, but she leaned back in her seat to wait.

I ran in, not bothering to knock, because I'd practically lived there before I moved away. Missy was sprawled on the brown vinyl couch, flicking through channels, a liter of Dr Pepper tucked in her arm. She muted the tube. "Hey! You got here fast."

"Yeah, there was no traffic for once. Here." I stuck the envelope of money between a dirty mug and an ashtray on the coffee table.

Missy gave me a sharp look and said, "You're in a hurry." I can never get anything past her.

I glanced out the window. "I got someone waiting in the car."

"You're turning red!" Missy sat up. "Who is she?"

"Just some girl."

Missy pulled back the curtain to peer out. "No way! The mighty Gabe is crushing."

"Missy." I gave her a begging look.

"Okay, okay. Let me get your stuff, and you can get back to your lady. You should have brought her in." Missy paused, examining my face. "She doesn't know, does she?"

I shrugged.

"Good girl, huh. Don't go breaking her heart, Gabe."

I scowled. I didn't have a thing to say to that, because I'd been a jerk to Missy's cousin Brit, and then her friend Sabrina, and Missy had never gotten over it. She refused to hook me up with anyone after that.

"Hold on a sec." Missy got the stuff, and we handled our business fast. Today it was e and some Oxies again, which fit fine in a vitamin bottle inside my jacket. I figured with the payoff from this load, I'd be ready to call the Craigslist people and make an offer on the car. I put everything away and told Missy thanks.

"No worries." She gave me a hard look. "Be nice to her."

I rolled my eyes—all girls were batting for the same team—and headed outside. The car was empty.

Every blood vessel in my body squeezed, and my breath dropped. *Fucking hoods, somebody snatched her!* I stood frozen for a second; then I ran down the driveway and into the street and yelled her name.

Nothing. Just a dog barking, and cars slicing by on Roxbury.

"Irina!" I yelled again. I fumbled in my pocket for my cell. I hadn't left her for more than five minutes. Should I call 9-1-1? I pictured some pimp thug dragging her by her hair into one of those nasty beat-downs, and . . . "Irina!" I yelled again. I ran a few steps one direction, then turned around and ran like an idiot the other way. "Irina!"

She came walking out of somebody's yard. "What?"

I stared at her. My heart was slamming.

"I was looking around," she said coolly.

"You were looking around," I repeated.

"Yeah. Next time don't leave me." She gave me her saltiest look and folded her arms across her chest. She had been trying to teach me a lesson.

"What the hell, Irina! You scared me!"

"Good," she said.

I was so mad, it wasn't safe to talk. I just stared at her and tried to force myself back to normal temperature. I'd been ready to bust into these sheds for her, take a bullet, whatever.

Irina got in the car. After a second, I followed her. "That was completely messed up," I said after slamming the door shut.

"I don't think it's very nice of you to leave me outside in a strange neighborhood while you do an errand," she said. "Is there a girl in there?"

"What? No! Or yeah, there's a girl, but it's not like that. She's just a friend." The idea of anything going on with Missy was so crazy, I couldn't even take it seriously. "I told you I had to drop something off. If I knew it was such a big deal, I would have had you come in."

"How do I know you're telling the truth?"

I threw open the car door. She was high maintenance. Girls that good-looking were always high maintenance. "Come on."

It was a bluff; most girls would have said, *No, baby, it's okay, I believe you*, but Irina got out and followed me, looking satisfied. I knocked on Missy's door again. It opened right away; I bet she'd been watching from behind the curtains.

I said, "Missy, my girl wants to meet you and make sure I'm not running some game."

Missy's eyes did the girl thing: zip, zap, up and down over Irina. She gave me a mischievous look. "Well, Gabe is a slut," she said matter-of-factly. "But I guess you probably know that."

Irina cocked her head. "No, I didn't know that. Tell me more."

"You should talk to my cousin Brit and my friend Sabrina."

"Missy!" I glared at her. "Quit messing with her. She's going to believe you." I turned to Irina. "She's just playing head games."

"Yeah, I'm just kidding," Missy said. "Gabe is not at *all* a player. You can totally trust him." And she fell apart, giggling.

"Is that right?" said Irina.

I grabbed her arm. "Let's go. Missy's completely screwing with you right now. We've been friends since fifth grade, and she loves to mess with me."

Missy nodded. "That's right. Don't believe anything I say." She widened her eyes. "I'm *such* a liar."

I practically hauled Irina down the steps, then turned to give Missy the evil eye. She called, "Just trying to warn her!"

Irina got back in the car and gave me a curious look. "Well, that was very informative."

I peeled out hard. "Don't let her get in your head. Missy loves to joke around."

"Hmm," said Irina. "Gabe, how many girls have you slept with?"

"What kind of question is that? Come on, Irina."

"An honest question, so give me an honest answer."

I stared straight ahead and drove faster. Bringing her here was the stupidest idea I'd ever had. "None. I'm a virgin."

"Don't insult my intelligence."

How many girls *had* I slept with? I wasn't sure. There had been lots of hookups at parties, starting in eighth grade. That was five whole years ago.

There was a long silence. Irina said, "Take me home. If you can't even be honest with me about that, we're not friends at all."

"I don't know," I said.

"You don't know how many people you've slept with?"

"No." I looked over at her. "Why are you here, anyway? You're obviously too good for me."

"What are you talking about?"

"You, Miss Perfect Straight-Edge Violin-Playing Russian Model. Why are you even wasting your time?" I sounded bitter; I didn't care.

Irina got a funny expression. "Well, because I like you, for one. I feel like there's somebody under there."

"Under *where*?"

"Under your cool veneer. Everybody lets their real self out sooner or later. Usually it takes about two months."

"Oh, you've got this worked out."

"I've dated a few jerks. Two months is how long it's always taken me to realize it. But I don't think you're a jerk. Just a player."

"Then why are you getting involved with me?"

"Because I can handle you." She gave me a cool look. "Now, are we going to get my ID or not?"

I chuckled, couldn't help it. *Cocky Russian.* I turned down a side street and started heading back. "Maybe I'll be the one handling you," I informed her.

She smiled. "We'll see about that."

♠ ♣ ♥ ♦

Damon's mom, Jennifer, lived in Mickey's Bar from when her shift at the DMV ended to whenever she: a) passed out; b) went home with somebody; c) got a fit of conscience and went hunting for Damon.

Mickey's was famous for being the biggest dive in Washington, and the regulars took pride in it. A few years ago, our old neighbor,

Joey, had T-shirts made that said "Mickey's Ain't for Mice" over a picture of a steaming vat labeled "Skunk Juice." Fran, the bartender, was famous for it. She kept a soup pot behind the bar where she dumped all the dregs from empties, and sometimes she threw in a little something top-shelf for flavor. It got people drunk fast and easy in a short time, which was a high priority at Mickey's. And it was only a dollar a shot.

I parked along the street outside the bar. You could see Irina was thinking twice as she got out. The sidewalk around Mickey's had big gaps in the concrete and a blanket of butts on the ground. The dirty white building was stuck between a video store and a taquería, and you wouldn't know it was a bar except for a sad little electric "Coors" sign hanging over the door.

"She lives *here*?" Irina said as I headed to the door.

"Well, she goes home to sleep. This is her bar. She always drinks here after work, and she's way more likely to hook up an ID for cheap if we catch her after a few beers."

"Are they going to let us in?"

"Yeah, they know me. My mom used to come here sometimes." I pushed open the door and held it for Irina.

Mickey's was a long rectangle with the bar against one wall, a pool table shoved into a corner, and an old-school jukebox loaded with Sammy Hagar, Zeppelin, and Whitesnake. Fran kept it dark in there, but there was no hiding the layers of dirt and the nappy carpet worn down to the threads. There were cardboard signs with "Skunk Juice, $1 a Shot" written in Sharpie, and some brown plastic stools lined up against the bar.

Def Leppard was playing on the jukebox, and Jennifer was leaning on the bar with a can of Bud Light, chatting with Fran. Fran was as yoked as a man, with curly red hair and blue eye shadow that looked like glitter pen. She was a big favorite with the biker dudes who sometimes stopped through. When we walked in, she and Jennifer stopped talking and stared at us.

Jennifer broke into a smile. "Gabe, good to see you. Where's your mom at?" Her eyes ran over Irina.

Fran didn't look as thrilled to see us. She folded her arms across her chest. "You know I can't have you in here."

"I just have to talk to Jennifer for a second."

Irina was looking nervous. I wished I could tell her to chill; this was just the dance we had to go through. Fran made a snorting noise and wandered down the bar, wiping it down with a rag that looked like its job was to make things dirty.

Jennifer gave me a knowing look and knocked back a swig of beer. "Don't even say it. I know what you're here for."

"Please?"

She chuckled. "Oh boy. You got them eyes."

"Come on, Jennifer, you know the laws in this country are messed up. We saved two hundred bucks."

She let the air out of her nose. "You know it's five bills, you little schemer." She looked at Irina. "How old are you, honey?"

"Seventeen," Irina said.

"And you know you can't trust this heartbreaker, right?"

Man! Thrown under the bus again! "Don't tell her that, Jennifer," I said. "That's messed up."

She sucked her teeth. "Oh, I ain't telling her. I'm warning her." She took another sip of beer and gave us a sparkling grin. "Don't fret. I'm just playing. I'll take care of you kids. When you wanna do it?"

This was the tricky part, because once Jennifer was parked at Mickey's, she didn't like to leave. "How about now? We'll drive you home, take the picture, and drop you back here in like twenty minutes." I pulled the cash from my pocket and held it out.

She took it and flicked through the bills. "You was so sure I'd say yes, weren't you? All right, honey, let's go." She heaved off her chair and waved at Fran. "Back in twenty. If Joe comes in, don't let him take my seat."

Fran tossed her dirty towel on the chair. "Reserved." Both women hooted with laughter.

♠ ♣ ♥ ♦

It didn't take long to get the picture taken. Jennifer promised to mail it soon, and we dropped her back off at Mickey's. Then Irina and I got on the I-5 heading toward her house. She had her window cracked even though it was freezing; she'd turned up Timati, and she had this amped-up, dangerous look in her eyes.

"You have to call me the second it comes," she said. "I cannot *wait* to go out."

I glanced at her and thought maybe it wasn't such a genius move, hooking up this model-hot girl with an ID. "As long as you take me for a bodyguard," I said, only half kidding. She giggled and tapped her fingers on my thigh, keeping the beat.

When we got to Irina's neighborhood, I pulled into Angel Point, a little grassy lookout three blocks from her house. Lake Sammamish glittered below us like metal, and you could see Mount Rainier cutting through the clouds. I turned to kiss her, but she put a hand on my chest and pushed me back.

"Gabe." Her brown eyes were serious. "I don't share my man."

I felt a jump of excitement. "You're worried about what Missy said?"

"I'm not worried. I'm just saying."

"You're saying I'm your man." I couldn't help the big grin that was coming out.

"Don't be cocky." She folded her arms across her chest and said coolly, "I'm saying . . . you're not *not* my man. But you certainly won't be if you go sleeping around while we're seeing each other."

"I would never."

She looked into my eyes. "Can I believe you?"

At that moment I decided, what the hell, I was going to be good. The woman of my dreams was giving me a chance. I'd had enough random sex that I could be done with it—for a while, at least, until I convinced her to quit with the waiting thing.

I took her hands in mine. She was so little and delicate, but I knew what kind of iron was under there now. I held her gaze. "I'm into you. There's nobody else. You're exactly what I want, and I'm not going to mess that up. Okay?"

She ducked her head. "You'd better not."

I thought what a jerk I'd been—all the times I'd said some bullshit like this. But this time it wasn't bullshit. I actually meant it.

"Irina, I won't." I kissed her as gently as I could, trying to show her I was for real.

It took her a minute, but she kissed me back, and left a chain of hungry kisses on my jaw. Then she climbed into my lap, pressing her forehead against mine and letting her hair fall in a tent around our faces. "Call me later," she said, then kissed me one more time, a long sexy one, and climbed out of the car.

I watched her walk away, the hair that had just been touching my face swinging back and forth. Then I looked up into the flat gray Seattle sky, and I felt like it reached up forever, and the whole world was exploding with goodness. I was capable of big things. I was the kind of guy a girl like her could fall for.

CHAPTER ELEVEN

I got Irina's ID in the mail, in an official DMV envelope. I'd just gotten home from school, and Mom wasn't around. I slit open the envelope with a knife and pulled out the card. Irina Petrova, age twenty-two. And a damn good picture, too. Thank you, Jennifer, and all other pissed-off government employees.

I texted Irina: *Got a present.* I couldn't wait to take her someplace fancy in Seattle, get real champagne, and go dancing at Deep Down or Re-bar.

I stared at my phone, waiting for her message back. We'd been texting constantly since the White Center trip. Irina didn't text like a normal person; she threw out these deep questions: *Have you ever been in love? Is there anything you'd die for?* I mean heavy stuff, on text!

I wondered if it was a Russian thing. Maybe that freezing-cold weather made them sit inside all day and just think. Actually, I liked it. I tried to give her real answers, although sometimes I got fresh with her—like *i want u* when she was trying to be deep.

I texted her again: *Pick u up at 8?* She still hadn't texted back, which was weird, but I thought maybe she was practicing and didn't see her phone. I started making a sandwich—Mom had been buying deli meat for Phil lately, and I was trying to eat it as fast as she could buy it—when my phone vibrated.

Please do not text, call, or otherwise have contact with Irina.
Mr. Petrova.

For a second I stood there, my cheeks going hot, my breath stuck.

Her parents had been spying. Of course they had. They were exactly the kind who would do that. Every private text I'd sent Irina flashed into my mind: talking about her face, her lips, her body, talking about how bad I wanted her.

No doubt they had her on complete lockdown now.

I threw my phone. I pictured her dad's beefy face and hard eyes and the way he'd looked at me, like *Hell no, not a chance.* He had it all dialed in: big job, beautiful wife, perfect daughter. I was just a low-life cockroach trying to bust into his palace, and now he was stepping on me.

I started pacing the kitchen. *What the—? Should I go there now?* No, there was nothing I could do. It was his property; he could call the cops. I'd have to wait for Irina to get hold of me. She'd figure that out, wouldn't she? Get online somehow and let me know what was up? But being homeschooled, she couldn't just borrow a friend's phone.

I could go crazy, picturing her locked up with no tech. They probably chained her to her violin. I took a step toward the door, then made myself stop. Going there would do nothing, maybe even make it worse. I had to wait. I slammed the counter with my hand and walked into the living room, leaving Phil's lunch meat on the counter.

My phone buzzed, and I jumped for it. It was only Tim giving me an update on a shipment of stuff he had coming in. Dude was getting on my nerves. I wasn't supposed to be deep in the game, just making connections for a few people, but Tim had some other guy involved now, a supplier he wanted me to meet. It was a big deal to him, so I figured I'd go along with it this once. I texted him back to set up a time, and then checked my messages in case something had come in the last half second.

It hadn't. I decided if I didn't hear from Irina by the weekend, I'd do something. I didn't know what, but something. That made me feel better, at least enough to get through the rest of the day.

♠ ♣ ♥ ♦

Next day, after school, which I'd spent mostly checking my phone for a text that didn't come, I headed to Forrest's with the guys. Forrest had the whole downstairs to himself: a bathroom, a living room, and a bedroom tricked out with leather furniture, a flat screen, and a dope gaming console. It was super clean in there (his family had a maid).

Kyle turned over some cash he owed me from his friend's party. Then we ate through half of Forrest's mini-fridge and settled down to our screens. Forrest started playing around in some virtual world, Kyle worked on college apps, Matt looked at college websites, and I surfed the net for a good English paper.

I was having a hard time concentrating because I couldn't stop thinking about Irina. Her house was about two miles from Forrest's, and I was going crazy knowing she was so close but I couldn't get to her. Couldn't she sneak out? Or just leave? I mean, she was almost eighteen. What were her parents going to do, physically stop her?

My phone buzzed and I ripped it out of my pocket before it was done moving.

Tim again, wanting to know if I could move some extra product. Man, he needed to chill. I decided I'd better answer him so he'd quit messing with my head, making me think it was Irina. It sounded like more product than I wanted to be handling, but it also sounded like official cash. And if Kyle could get rid of it as fast as he had the last batch . . .

I looked at Kyle and said, "My friend's got some stuff coming in next week."

Forrest turned around. "What kind?" His voice was way too eager.

Matt looked up, frowning.

"Yeah, what kind?" Kyle said absentmindedly, still typing on his computer.

"Just some e," I said. That wasn't true. There were also Oxies, the good old kind with no time release, and some designer dope.

"Can you hook up Oxies, too?" Forrest asked.

I shook my head.

Forrest narrowed his eyes. "Dude, you could if you wanted to. You got those bottles for Kyle. Those were high quality."

"I thought those were for your Overlake friends," I said to Kyle. Kyle looked confused. "Yeah, mostly. But Forrest likes them, too, so I gave him some. What? Why you looking at me like that?"

Damn. I was pissed at them and myself.

"What's wrong, man?" Kyle brushed his hair out of his eyes. He hated people to be mad at him.

I turned to Forrest. *He* knew what was wrong. People with the sickness know it's inside them, like a curled-up tiger. And Forrest was feeding it. Somehow he knew—and he knew I knew—that I didn't think he needed to be playing with Oxies.

I didn't answer Kyle, just kept staring at Forrest. "How much are you using, anyway? Oxies aren't e. They're pretty fucking addictive."

He immediately got defensive, which was a bad sign. "I don't know! Not a lot! What are you, my dad?"

"I'm not your dad, and I think it's a good question," Matt said quietly. "How much are you using?"

"Back off, Matt!" snapped Forrest.

Kyle looked from Matt to me to Forrest, and I saw his gears clicking. He said, "Chill, Forrest. They're just looking out. Remember when Chad Dougherty got hooked on pain pills or something stupid? Didn't they make him do one of those wilderness programs?"

That broke the tension, and Forrest gave a half smile. "Oh man, yeah, they did. He had to climb ropes up a mountain or something. And he had to eat protein bars and water for a month. Remember how skinny he was when he got back?"

The awkward moment was over, and I went back to looking for my English paper. I'd found a good one, but I couldn't concentrate on it; my brain was stuck on Forrest. I was having one of those horrible moments when you realize you've been doing something bad and you have to change.

All the reasons I shouldn't stop hooking up people jumped into my mind. Forget taking Irina anywhere nice like I'd been imagining. No more clothes. No more going out to lunch. No more fun. People would be pissed. It's not cool when your connection steps out of the game. I would lose the status I'd built up.

But mostly, I would be poor.

The past month was the first time in my life I'd felt okay about cash. Mom was always blowing her paychecks buying her friends drinks or getting tickets to see some moldy old band. We'd start the month eating takeout, and by the last week we were down to ramen. It used to scare me when I was little. Then as I got older, I realized everything always turned out okay. But it's hard to shake that anxious feeling that you might not have enough food.

Why not sell dope and make bank? Alcohol and cigarettes were legal, and so were pain meds, and people got hooked on those all the time. Why let the government make all the money? Drugs messed people up; I knew that. But I always thought, just like with booze, if people kept their use under control, it was okay.

The problem was, fiends were the best customers. And there was no telling who they were. No telling who was a potential fiend, even. People had mad head trips going on, or maybe bad genes, that made them ripe for getting hooked on something. So dealing was like shooting into a crowd. I'd never know who I'd hit.

Maybe I'd hit someone like Forrest.

I glanced at him. His shaggy head was hunched over the computer, his nose almost touching the screen. He was very cool, but he had a weird emptiness to him, like he was half-bored, half-pissed. The exact type to get addicted.

Yeah, I had to get out of the game.

I made myself scan the *Hamlet* paper. It was solid, but not too good, so they might believe I wrote it. I punched my card numbers into the PayPal account, hit "Buy." When my transaction went through, I logged out and stood up. Forget waiting for the weekend. I needed to see Irina now.

"I have to bolt. See you guys later." I grabbed my bag and started for the door.

Kyle looked up. "I thought we were going to watch the game."

"I got something to handle."

He cocked his head. "Irina?"

I couldn't help it; I turned red. The guys were always giving me a hard time for texting with her so much. They said she had me on a short chain.

Kyle raised a hand. "Go on, little dog. Your owner's calling."

I flipped him off as I opened the door. "If you could get a woman that fine to talk to you, you'd be putting on your own leash."

He chuckled. "I probably would. I probably would."

I had just gotten down the driveway when I heard the house door open behind me. "Gabe!" Matt called. He didn't have his shoes on, but he came down the steps and picked his way across the gravel.

I opened my car and tossed my backpack in the backseat. "What's up?"

Matt was looking uneasy. "Listen . . ." He stared off past my shoulder and shifted his weight. I breathed out a cloud of cold air and waited for him to say whatever it was he needed to say. "I've known Forrest since kindergarten. He's been through some stuff. He doesn't need what you're selling, okay?"

"I know, dude. I'm trying *not* to sell to him. Didn't you hear me in there?"

Matt finally looked right at me, and his eyes, usually so mellow, were bright with anger. "Why do you have to sell to anyone?"

I didn't answer. But I thought, *Because I need money.*

"Never mind. Just don't sell to Forrest, okay? No matter what he says." Matt turned away and walked back toward the house.

I stared after him. Normally I'd be pissed that somebody was up in my business. But I almost wanted to call Matt back and explain myself. I cared what he thought. He was a good dude, and I knew he was just looking out for his friend. But the door closed behind him, and I got in my car.

♠ ♣ ♥ ♦

I peeled out and drove down Forrest's driveway, which was practically a road by itself. I turned onto Remington and flew through the backstreets to Irina's place, the hours of stress—Matt, Forrest, Irina—boiling together until I was turbocharged, ready to kick down the door. I parked a few houses away.

Then my brain started working again. What was I going to do, storm her house? There was a car in the driveway—probably her mom's. The charged feeling began to drain out of me.

But I wasn't waiting anymore. I looked around, didn't see anybody, and ran around the house into the back. Her yard was buzz-cut, edged with bushes that looked like they wouldn't dare put a leaf out of line. The bricks were dark red and perfectly clean;

no moss or ivy. I wondered what it had been like for her, growing up in this place.

I eased along the side of the house until I was about where I thought Irina's room should be. There was only one window with lace curtains. I stared up at it for a while.

Now what? I'd heard of people throwing rocks, but that seemed like a great way to get caught or break the glass. I looked at the drainpipe—it was thick and solid—and then at the balcony on the room next to Irina's. I'd always been good at ropes in gym class.

Was I really thinking this? The worst that could happen would be that her parents called the cops, but more likely Mr. Petrova would try to kick my ass himself—if he was home. And I didn't think he was. Plus I was a good runner.

I pushed up my sleeves and hit the drainpipe. It screeched and dumped some nasty leaves on me, but I was fast. In a minute I was on the balcony. I put my face against the glass and tried to peer through the curtains. I could see the outlines of furniture, but no movement. I tried the handle. It was locked. I bet I could jimmy it. It was a crappy second-story porch door, anyway. I broke out my card and opened it in a second.

My heart was slamming as I stepped inside. It smelled a little musty, and all the furniture was heavy and dark and expensive-looking. I walked through the room, feeling insanely awake, every creak of the floor like a gunshot. There's something about being in somebody's house when you're not supposed to that's exciting and terrifying at the same time.

I opened the door and slid into the hall. I heard a clank down-stairs and froze. Someone fooling with pots in the kitchen.

A couple more steps and I was at Irina's door. If she was there, and I walked in, she might scream. But I couldn't exactly knock. I pushed in the handle to make it quieter, turned it slowly, and cracked the door. She was lying on her bed, asleep.

I slid in and locked the door. There was this feeling in my throat, almost choked up. I could have stared at her for a while, her hair spread out, her skin so pale I could see blue lines around her forehead. She was wearing sweats and a T-shirt, and she looked so beautiful, I wanted to just sit by her bed and let her keep sleeping. But who knew how much time we had?

I shook her gently. "Irina."

Her eyes flew open, and she gasped.

"Shhh." I put my finger on her lips. "I came up the drainpipe and in from the balcony."

She pulled me into her arms and kissed me hard. She said something in Russian, and it was so sexy, I would have done a bid for breaking and entering just to hear it again. I lay on top of her and we kissed for a while, and it was hot and sweet and everything in between.

Then she put both hands on my cheeks and looked me in the eyes and whispered, "You're crazy."

"I know," I whispered back.

"You can't stay. My mom is home."

"How come you didn't text me or something?"

"I couldn't! My dad was so mad, he threw my phone in the toilet! They won't let me online."

"He read all our texts?"

"Yes. I told them we didn't do anything, but they don't believe me. They think we're sleeping together," she said bitterly.

"That's pretty crazy, because you're the straightest girl I ever met," I said. She looked upset, so I brushed her hair off her face and changed the subject. "How long do they have you on lockdown?"

"Until I'm done applying to conservatories in December. They think it's your fault I haven't been playing well lately. They said you're distracting me. Even when I'm done applying, I'm not supposed to talk to you again."

I stared at the wall, trying to stay cool. Irina had enough on her plate without me losing my temper. "That's messed up. They don't even know me," I said finally.

"I know. I hate them." She said it so coldly, it was almost scary. "I can't do this anymore. I'm going crazy." She glanced at me. "Let me stay at your house for a while."

"*Really?*" I said. "I mean, yeah, we could do that. My mom wouldn't care or anything. But would your parents, like, call the cops?"

"Maybe." Irina sounded so sad, I wished I hadn't said anything, just taken our chances.

I tried to backtrack. "Who cares? Let's do it. You're almost eighteen anyway."

"No, it's not worth it. I don't want to get your mom involved." Irina squeezed my hand. "Can you come back this weekend? Friday? With a ladder?"

"With a—are you for real?"

She nodded, looking fierce. It was an expression I was getting to know. "Yeah, put it against my window at midnight. I'll climb out."

"Couldn't you sneak out the door or go down the drainpipe or something?" I wasn't trying to be weak, but a ladder seemed a little risky.

"We have an alarm system and all the doors are rigged. Second-floor windows aren't, though."

"Um, are you sure it won't set off the alarm?"

"Are you scared?"

"No. I'll be there." I kissed her, taking my time. The way we were moving, we could have been making love.

Finally she forced me back and sat up, looking red in the face. "You should go before my dad gets home."

I grinned at her. "Your husband's going to be one lucky dude."

She went to her door, opened it, and peeked in the hall. "Come on." Her sweats hung low on her hips. I would have given anything to stay a while longer.

We walked fast through the guest room and she stood on the balcony and kissed me again. "Romeo, Romeo," she said, and broke up giggling. "I can't believe you climbed a drainpipe."

I kissed her neck. "I'd do more than that to get to you."

She held my hands and looked at me with happy eyes. "See you Friday."

"Friday," I said, and climbed down that nasty pipe. As I ran through her backyard, I thought that in a weird way, her dad had done me a favor. Irina seemed even more passionate now.

CHAPTER TWELVE

Sessions with Mr. Newport were killing me. He was prepping me for the final, which was coming next week, and I was worried I was going to blow it to hell. I didn't know how Bs in science at Jefferson translated to "don't know jack about science" at Claremont. But I hadn't given up yet.

Wednesday, the day after seeing Irina, I pushed open the door, and Newport looked up from his computer. His desk was messier than most people's lockers. It was buried under about fifty pounds of paper, dirty mugs, and Post-its. He smiled. "Hi, Gabe!"

"Hey, Mr. Newport." I dropped my bag and sat across from him.

He put his laptop on the floor and swept his arm across his desk like a plow, clearing a space between us. Then he fished through the stacks on his desk and pulled out some brochures. "Take a look at these."

I looked. Colleges spent a lot of money on those things. Big pictures of shiny weight equipment and giant pools and classrooms that look like doctors' offices. Kids smiling way too hard. At least one black, Asian, and Latino kid in every picture. I opened up one and pretended to look through.

Mr. Newport lowered his curly head, trying to meet my eyes. "I don't want to be nosy, but Ms. Tacquard told me that you still haven't taken the SAT. That's something you should have done last year. But there's still time. We can get you signed up for a test this month, and you can get some applications in." He patted the brochures. "I'll help you through the process."

I stared at the Olympic rings on his desk from too many hot coffee mugs. I almost didn't have the guts to tell him, but I made myself push through it. "I'm not going to college. Didn't Ms. T. tell you that?"

Mr. Newport did the head thing again—dip, force me to look at him—and said, "Gabe." His voice was strong, and his eyes were on fire. Damn, this was why he got that education degree. "Don't talk that way. You're a smart kid, I can tell. I think you've had a bad hand in terms of your prior education, but that doesn't have to hold you back." He tapped his head. "You've got the ability. The rest is just makeup work."

His eyes were blazing so hard they got my attention. What if he was right? I mean, sometimes I did feel smart. Or at least, not dumb. I had good ideas, I got jokes quickly, I remembered stuff easy if I could say it out loud. But the reading and writing thing . . . Why couldn't I get it right? I almost wanted to ask him, but I didn't want him to change his mind about me being smart.

Mr. Newport put his elbows on the desk. "Did you know that over the course of a lifetime, college graduates make more than twice as much as high school graduates?"

"Really?" I said.

He nodded. "And they're way more likely to get jobs. But it's not just the money. Education opens your mind. It gives you a chance to invent yourself."

Education does *not* open your mind; it channels your mind into the little path that all the adults have picked for you. But the part about inventing myself got to me. Because I'd thought before about how I'd like to just shake off my life and invent myself into somebody else. Maybe to do that, you had to play the game, get the gold stars on your chart, let yourself be brainwashed a little, and then you could do what you wanted with your life.

Maybe I just hadn't tried hard enough.

"I'll think about it," I said.

Mr. Newport smiled. "Good! That's great. And I'm going to support you all the way. First we need to get you signed up for the SAT."

"No, first we need to get me to pass your final."

He laughed. "You're going to pass. You know a lot of this stuff cold. But you're right, let's buckle down." He bent over my book.

The thing he didn't realize was that I was doing good because we were talking, and I didn't have to read anything. But I knew those bubbles would screw me up like always. Still, when Mr. Newport got done with his cheerleading, I walked out feeling sort of charged up. Dude was like the Pied Piper of Education.

♠ ♣ ♥ ♦

The next day I had my meeting with Tim and his supplier. I'd kept thinking I should cancel, but I never sent the text, and now it was too late. Had I really gone straight-arrow about the Forrest thing? A few days later, and the logic was feeling fuzzy. Why was he *my* problem? He wasn't a little kid; he could make his own decisions. Maybe I'd do just this one last batch, keep it far away from him, and then quit.

Or maybe I wouldn't. I wanted to take Irina somewhere really nice when she was off grounding, and I wanted that new car. I had enough cash for it, but it would almost clean me out. Better to build more of a cushion.

I drove to White Center, parked in front of Missy's house, and took the steps two at a time. A rusted rake was leaning against the door; Missy's dad must have been making his annual stab at the lawn. I put my hand on the knob, then thought better of it and knocked. I didn't want this Jay dude to think I was the law and do something rash.

The curtain moved, Tim peered at me through the dirty glass, and a second later the door opened. "Hey." Tim slapped my hand and stepped aside to let me through. He looked over his shoulder. "Jay, this is my man, Gabe."

Jay was sitting on the couch. He raised a hand. He was tanned with shaggy blond hair, sporting jeans and a hoodie. He had one of those open friendly faces, like Kyle's, the kind of face you automatically trust. His feet were kicked up on the coffee table.

"Hey, bro, you're doing a pretty good trade on the Eastside. Thanks for the business." His eyes were wide and blue.

"I'm doing okay."

"More than okay. You like living over there?"

"It's all right."

Jay tipped his head back on the couch. "They got better restaurants over there than even downtown. Sometimes me and my girlfriend go there to eat, even though the traffic sucks." He made a face.

"Yeah? Where do you go that's good?"

"There's this one Mexican place, La Casa Bonita, that makes mad fajitas. And they got this homemade salsa that's, like, gringo beware."

I smiled. "I'll have to check it out sometime."

There was a pause, and Jay and Tim traded looks. Jay nodded at the coffee table. "I got a lot of product in there. You interested in stepping up sales at all?"

There was a gray backpack sitting on a stack of *TV Guides*. I picked it up and asked, "Okay if I take a look?" Jay nodded. I unzipped the pouch and checked the contents. Bags of e, bottles of Oxies, and some blue pills I didn't recognize. I held one up and looked at him.

"It's 2CB. Party drug, goes for fifteen or twenty a pill. Doesn't last as long as e, but a similar high."

My brain started ticking. There were two or three thousand in profits in that bag, easy. It would put me over the edge from okay to comfortable, and I could get my ride with no worries. Forrest's face popped into my head for a second, but I ignored it. I couldn't be making business decisions based on somebody else's bad choices.

"It'll probably take me a month," I said, turning back to Jay.

Tim frowned. "You can do it faster than that, can't you? Come on, Gabe. I told him you were up for it."

"Why does it matter?" I asked.

Jay shrugged. "It doesn't. A month is fine."

But Tim was giving me a begging look. I bet he had something invested, and the more product I moved, the more cash he got, and the more he could stuff back in his own veins. I ran a hand over the backpack. It was loaded tight.

"How much?" I asked.

"I'll give you the whole kit for fifteen hundred," said Jay.

Cheaper than I'd thought. With Claremont prices, I could make bank and take Irina to the restaurant in the Space Needle. I'd always wanted to go there.

I sorted the contents, and it was all straight. I counted out the money and set it on the table.

Jay said thoughtfully, "You know, if you want more than that, just say the word."

"Nah, this is cool for now. I don't know how long I'm going to stay in the game."

"What are you talking about?" Tim demanded.

"I'm just not trying to do a bid. Dealers always get busted eventually." I gave him a look. "So do addicts."

"What are you trying to say, man?" He ran his fingers through his hair. "Jay never would've wanted to meet you if he knew you were pulling out. Don't be weak, Gabe."

"I never said I was pulling out. I just said I don't know long I'm staying in the game." I gave Tim an annoyed look.

Jay unfolded himself from the couch. Dude was well over six feet. He jerked his neck, cracking it. "Chill, Tim. He can do whatever he wants." He turned to me. "You're in charge. Sell this stash, and if you decide you're done, you're done, no worries. But if you want to stay in the game, we got plenty more where this came from. Cool?"

He looked so mellow that I felt better. But my gut was saying to leave the backpack on the table and get out.

I've never been that good at listening to my gut, though. I picked up the sack, nodded at both of them, and said, "Peace."

Driving back to Redmond, I had this messed-up feeling, like I drank too much coffee, kind of sick and wired and pissed at the same time. The backpack felt like a grenade in the trunk with the pin pulled out.

I tried to focus on how much cash I was set to make. How comfortable I'd be now. Maybe it was time to do something big, reward myself. Like get that Altima.

Yeah, time to pull the trigger.

♠ ♣ ♥ ♦

The car people lived a little north of Bellevue on one of those winding roads with lots of trees. The lady who answered the door was tiny and red-haired, a leprechaun lady, with a little kid peeking from behind her and a baby hanging in a sling in front. She had that wiped-out look that moms of little kids always have. When I'd called earlier to set up the meeting, she'd sounded so thrilled that I knew I could do some lowballing.

She waved me toward the garage. "It's in there. It's in perfect condition. We got the SUV for these guys." She looked down at the kid wrapped around her legs. "The keys are on the front seat if you want to take it for a test drive. Take as long as you want."

I didn't need long. My buddy Mike's dad was a mechanic, and back in elementary school, he'd taught us everything about engines, upkeep, and the rest. He let us practice on the cars he repaired, and we used to hammer around in engines with screwdrivers and stuff. One time a customer caught us at it, and Mike's dad said he needed us for our "small hands." Anyway, I knew what I was looking for, and the lady was telling the truth: the car was in perfect condition. I took it around the block twice. It was no Nissan GT-R, which was what I really wanted, but it was a fine car, nothing to be ashamed of.

I knocked on her door again, and she opened it, looking hopeful. "It seems okay," I said. "This is all I got. If you want it, I'll buy the car today." I handed her an envelope I'd gotten ready with the amount written on it. It was a lot less than she was asking, but it would leave me with the cushion I wanted. And there's nothing like the sight of straight bills to get people in a negotiating mood.

She counted it. "I'll have to call my husband."

"That's cool," I said. But I was nervous while she dialed. This was where it could fall apart; he was a dude, and he wasn't looking at the cash. Two strikes.

I was in luck: he didn't answer. The woman put down the phone, brushed her hair out of her eyes, and jiggled the baby, looking totally unsure. "Can we call you later?"

I kept eye contact. "Nah, I need to know now."

She sighed. "Okay. I want to get it off my hands. But you're getting a great deal," she said accusingly.

I kept my face cool and handed her the envelope, no victory dance until I was outside.

She gave me the keys and fished the title out of a drawer. "I'll sign this over to you now, but is it all right if my husband handles the rest of the paperwork later?"

"Sure. Can I leave my old car parked out front for the night?"

She smiled. "I don't own the sidewalk."

I took that magic paper, and those beautiful keys, and walked as calmly as I could out to my new ride. I emptied my old trunk into my new trunk, slid into the leather bucket seat, and pushed in the key. The engine purred like a lion.

As I drove away, blasting Roots, air coming in the windows clean and cold, the trip to Tim's started to fade. The bass was strong and powerful, and the interior smelled like leather. I decided I was being too hard on myself. Of course I was in this game; look what I'd just gotten out of it. I tested the gearshift and switched to third. I'd always wanted a manual—gears meant you were really driving.

♠ ♣ ♥ ♦

I hadn't meant to tell Mom about the car right away; I needed to come up with a good story first. But she and Phil were standing on the step saying good-bye when I pulled up. It made me sick to see them hugging. Phil wasn't much taller than Mom, but he was about twice as wide, and I could see the bald spot on his head.

There was an awkward moment when they looked at my car, looked at each other, and then looked at me. Phil didn't bother saying hi, just ducked his head and hurried past me on the way to his Benz.

Mom waited on the step, her eyebrows up. "That's a nice car."

"Yeah, I've been saving up." I tried for casual, but it came out nervous.

"Gabe, where did you get the money for that?"

"Working!" I pushed past her and thumped up the stairs. I was hungry, but I didn't stop at the fridge. The only way to escape was to pretend to do homework.

But Mom was a bulldog. She followed me, and when I tried to hit my room, she said, "Gabe, look at me."

Crap.

I looked at her, and her green eyes were *loving* in this horrible way that made me feel sick with guilt. "Yeah."

"I wasn't born yesterday. I've noticed the new clothes and the fancy phone."

I fiddled with my shirt—I would have fiddled with air if there wasn't anything else. I couldn't look at her.

"You're not working that much. Tell me the truth, Gabe."

"The truth is, the car looks nice, but it needs a lot of work," I lied. "It was cheap. I couldn't drive the other one anymore. You know how bad it was. And people tip a lot around here."

Mom didn't say anything, just stared at me, searching my face. I felt like the worst jerk in the universe. Mom was always being lied to by guys, and I'd promised myself I wasn't going to ever be one of them. And now here I was, lying worse than all of them put together. Because this would hurt her even more than getting cheated on.

"Really?" she said softly.

"Yeah." I could barely get it out.

"You'd come to me if you needed money, not try to make it some . . . illegal way?"

I nodded.

"Okay, honey." She hugged herself. "Okay, I believe you." She sounded like she was trying to convince herself.

I turned to go, and she said, "What about insurance?"

"I'll transfer the policy," I said.

"It's probably going to be more . . ." She trailed off.

Phil had been paying our bills for a while now. She was saying, in code, that he might not appreciate the price hike.

"I'll pay it myself," I said.

"Well, call and see how much it is, and maybe I can talk—"

I cut her off. "I'll pay it myself."

CHAPTER THIRTEEN

A s I pulled the ladder—borrowed from Missy's boyfriend—out of my trunk on Friday night, I was jumpy. Dude with an extension ladder strolling around a rich neighborhood at midnight? If cops were patrolling, it was game over.

But there wasn't a body on the street as I walked to Irina's. I moved fast, ducked through the hedge and around the back, keeping away from the house. All the lights were off, and the moon was hidden behind clouds. It was black, and the air was so wet, it felt like cold hands. Ghost weather.

I extended the ladder, and it screeched, sending my heart rocketing. But I waited to the count of ten, and nothing happened. At the top of that thing was Irina. I put my hand on the first rail and just about died, because there was a creak above me.

Her window opening.

I could see her dark shape squeezing out, foot waving around for a spot. I hoped she knew what she was doing. Girls can be stupid at stuff like sneaking out.

Every step Irina took sounded like boards breaking, or maybe I was just paranoid. I kept remembering when she said her dad would be the only Russian dude to shoot me.

When she got down, her eyes were shining in the dark, and she had a big, amped grin. She kissed me once, hard, on the mouth. Then she whispered, "Come on," and grabbed my hand.

I shook my head and pulled the ladder off the wall, collapsed it, and stuck it in some bushes. That's the kind of detail that gets you caught.

Then we were gone. We got rash once we were on the sidewalk, giggling and running, even though our footsteps were loud, but all I cared about was her hand in mine and the feeling that we were busting out of jail.

She pulled me into her neighbor's yard a few doors down. The lawn was huge, the house was set way back on the lot, and there were tons of trees. But it was still somebody's place.

"What about Angel Point?" I said.

"That's too far. Don't worry, they're asleep." She pushed me against a tree and—dang. She was feeling bad, all right. We kissed hard and hungry for a while, and I was just about thinking she was done with the "waiting" thing, when she pushed me back and tugged down her shirt and said, "Okay."

It hurt to hear that. I kissed her neck and whispered, "Come on," and some other sweet things, but she got stubborn and pulled away and sat down in the wet grass.

I sighed and sat next to her. "Are you for real? 'Cause I don't know if I can take this."

"I don't know if I can, either," she said.

"Then why are you doing it?"

"I already told you."

I leaned back against the tree. Good thing it was wet and freezing, because I needed a cold shower. "Does God want you to torture guys?"

"Probably not," she said, sounding miserable. "I don't really know what's okay to do and what isn't. I mean, there's a lot of stuff other than sex we can do . . . but then it's just frustrating."

"I'm surprised your parents haven't laid it out for you," I said sarcastically, because I *was* frustrated.

"They're not religious. I'm sort of trying to figure this out for myself."

"They're not?" I said. Every time I thought I had Irina pegged, she surprised me.

She picked up a twig and twirled it in her fingers. "No. It sort of skipped a generation. My great-grandpa was a priest, but my grandma and my mom aren't religious at all."

"He was probably too strict. You know what they say about preachers' kids."

"That's not it," she said softly. "My great-grandpa went to the Gulag for being a priest. It scared my grandma, and she raised my mom with no religion because she thought it would keep her safe."

"What's the Gulag?" I asked.

"A system of concentration camps." The words hung in the night, heavy and cold.

I felt a chill down my back. "Like the Nazis?"

"Yeah, but in Russia. Stalin had lots of them. One of the big points of communism was to get rid of religion, so they sent tons of priests and nuns to the Gulag. Kids were supposed to report their parents if they read the Bible or anything." Irina snapped the twig and let the pieces drop. "In the schools, they gave kids playing cards with the Trinity on them, to, you know, make fun of it."

"That's creepy," I said.

"Yeah, really creepy. My great-grandpa wrote letters from the Gulag, and we still have them. He spent eight years in there before he died."

I touched her hand. "I'm sorry."

She slid her fingers through mine. "It's okay."

"Have you read his letters?"

"Yeah. There were some poems he wrote and love letters for my great-grandma. He talked about trusting God and loving their enemies. It's what got me interested in going to church, actually."

I didn't know what to say. This stuff was heavy. Finally I joked, "A lot of kids drop out of church to mess with their parents. I guess you did the opposite."

She smiled. "Yeah. I didn't do it on purpose to mess with them, though. And they don't really mind. They think people should decide for themselves about religion."

"When did you start going?"

"A couple years ago. My friend Anya's family went every Sunday, and I spent the night at her house a lot, so I'd just go with them. It's so beautiful. It's like . . ." She trailed off. "It's hard to describe. It's the oldest kind of Christianity, and it's . . . mysterious. At first I went because I loved the music so much. Then Anya's mom gave me a Bible and I started reading it, and it helped me with some things."

"Like what?"

She paused, and I thought maybe she wasn't going to tell me. "Okay, like before big concerts? I sometimes get these panic things." She darted me a quick look. "Like I start obsessing about how I'm going to play, and then I can't breathe right. But the Bible says we're not supposed to make a big deal of ourselves, or go after earthly honors. I feel like that's what I've been doing my whole life: going after honors. It was nice to hear I didn't have to."

"That's cool." I pulled her closer. "I'm glad it helped you not stress. Because you're amazing even if you never play the violin again. You're not, like, a pair of hands to play the violin. You're *you*."

She leaned her head on my shoulder, and she felt so good and warm in my arms. "You're deep," I said, kissing her head.

"I guess that's better than shallow." She smiled up at me. "Let's not talk about me anymore. I'm boring. I want to know more about you. What's your family like?"

I gave a half laugh. "Messed up." I really didn't want to talk about my family. How come girls always got nosy?

"Come on, Gabe. You've met my family, and I don't even know anything about yours. They can't be worse than my parents."

"It's not *they*. It's just my mom," I told her.

"Well, but don't you get to see your dad on weekends or anything?" she asked.

"I don't even know who my dad *is*." It just came out, and instantly I wished I hadn't said it.

Irina said quietly, "Your mom never told you?"

"She doesn't know, either. I guess she was seeing a couple guys back when she got pregnant with me, and none of them were any good." My pulse was going faster. *Why am I telling her this?*

Irina didn't say anything, just picked up my hand and kissed it.

In the quiet, I heard a low sound. A motor. I froze. It was going slower than any car should, and that meant either a cop or a drive-by. In this hood, it had to be a cop. "Shhh," I whispered.

The car slid by and pulled to a stop about twenty feet from us.

Irina's fingers closed on my arm, stiff as bone.

"Be cool," I whispered. My mind was flying. They had to be here for us—no other reason they'd stop in front of this house. Somebody had heard us. I glanced over, and sure enough, there was a square of light in one of the windows of the house.

The car door opened and a flashlight beam swung wide of us, playing over empty grass. I'd dealt with cops before, and I knew we had about one minute to make our move.

"I'll distract him," I said in her ear. "You run. You can pull the ladder through your window. I'll meet you . . ." I thought about it. If he threw me in juvie for trespassing, they wouldn't hold me longer than a day. There was no room in those places. "Monday night at midnight."

"You'll get in trouble!" Irina said under her breath.

There was the crunch of footsteps on grass, and the beam moved closer.

I squeezed her hand. "Go!" I jumped to my feet, ran across the lawn, kicked over a planter, and pounded as hard as I could down the sidewalk.

The cop shone his light on me and yelled, "Freeze!" Something metal clicked.

I stopped and threw my hands in the air. I wasn't trying to get shot.

Irina's footsteps were loud, and the cop turned for half a second, but decided to stick with the sure thing. He ran up to me, gun out, and barked, "Don't move." He was a young cop, in pretty good shape. A white dude—that was lucky. Might cut me some slack. Lights clicked on behind me, and I could see dark outlines of people looking out the windows.

I stood up straight and said, "I'm sorry, Officer. I was meeting my girlfriend. We shouldn't have been here, but she was afraid her parents would see her if we stayed at her house."

He ignored me. "I'm going to pat you down. Keep your arms high."

I stayed still as he searched me. "That was the girl who ran away?" He ran his hands down my sides.

"Yes, sir. Please let her go. Her parents are crazy strict, and she's been grounded for a long time. We just missed each other, is all."

The cop let out a snort. "Tomcatting. I did the same thing when I was your age. What's your name?"

"Gabriel James, sir."

"Age?"

"Seventeen."

"Address?"

I rattled it off.

"Got an ID?"

"It's in my car, sir. About two blocks from here."

"Where does your girlfriend live?"

I pointed down the street vaguely. "Sir, please. Her parents would ground her for a year if they knew she sneaked out. We weren't even doing anything. You can do whatever you want to me, but please just let her go."

The cop looked into my eyes. After a second, he said, "All right. I like that you're willing to take the heat for your girlfriend. Do you know you were trespassing on private property?"

"Yes, sir. I'm sorry," I said.

"I need to speak with the owners. I'm going to have you wait in the car."

The cop let me into the back. I'd been in the wrong end of a cop car once before, when me and Tommy Fanning got busted tagging Watawa Grocery. They'd taken us to juvie, booked us, and let us out that same night when our parents came.

"Wait here," the cop told me, shutting the door. I heard the click of the lock. I watched as he walked up the driveway, meeting a man in a bathrobe halfway down. They talked for a few minutes, and then the cop came back and got in the car.

He talked to me through the glass as he started the engine. "You're lucky he's not pressing charges. I'm going to drive you to your car and follow you home. I want to have a word with your parents. That had better be your address."

"It is, sir."

"Which way?"

I pointed.

He pulled into the street. "Don't get that girl pregnant, understand? It's not a joke for her."

"That's not going to happen," I said. "She won't even give it up, sir."

He laughed. "Good for her."

I switched the subject, because I was afraid he might ask her name. "How long have you been a police officer?"

"Three years."

"Do you like it?"

"Yeah, I like it okay," he said. "The only bad part is everybody thinks we're jerks."

"People should be glad you're protecting them," I said. Of course I was blowing smoke; I'd always hated the po-po myself. But this guy seemed all right.

He half turned, glancing back at me. "People just see us as the guys who hand out tickets. My wife makes friends, and when they hear she's married to a cop, they back off."

"That sucks," I said.

"Is this your car?" He slowed next to my ride, the only one parked on the curb.

"Yeah, that's it."

We stopped, and the officer got out and opened my door. "Okay, let's see that ID."

I took my license out of the glove box, and he scanned it into a handheld thing that looked like an iPhone. After a minute he looked up. "You're clear. Get in your car and I'll follow you home."

I got in. Mom was going to freak when I came home with a police escort. At least Irina had gotten away. I drove slow and easy, using my turn signal like thirty feet before I needed to. I sat rod-straight in my seat. When we got to Remington, the cop car pulled up next to me and the officer rolled down his window. *Crap.* I'd done something wrong, broken some traffic rule I didn't know about. I rolled down my window.

"Stay out of trouble, Gabe." He raised a hand and pulled away.

I stared after him. *He's letting me off?*

His taillights disappeared around the corner. *He is!*

I wanted to scream *Thank you!* Maybe I had been too harsh about cops. Guess if I was getting carjacked, I'd want one around. Or knifed. Or robbed. There were plenty of reasons for cops to exist, come to think of it.

CHAPTER FOURTEEN

Saturday and Sunday I spent locked up studying, until I was ready to punch the wall. Damn words kept squishing together, especially on the left side. I kept thinking if I could just concentrate, it would be okay, but it never was. It took me like twenty minutes to get through each page, and even then I only understood some of it. I was starting to feel nauseated.

But I kept at it. Finals were next week, and I had to pass them. No screwing around with summer school. I had this feeling that things with me and Irina were only just starting. I'm not saying the *m* word—that wasn't even in my vocabulary—I'm just saying I couldn't imagine liking any girl better.

So I sat at my desk and studied telomeres until they were sweating out my pores and I was seeing diagrams of cells even when I closed my eyes. I couldn't believe Kyle and Matt and Forrest did this every day.

My mom poked in her head to say good night and about fell over when she saw me with a book open. "Oh, Gabe! Good job, honey!" she said in this shocked, delighted voice.

"Are you going to bed?" I asked.

"Well, I was going to, but do you need anything? I could make you a sandwich."

I pretended to think about it. "Yeah, a strawberry milk shake from Dairy Queen, some McDonald's fries, and a big Wendy's burger."

Mom sighed. "Well, it's a little late, but you know what? You're doing such a—"

I started laughing. "Mom! I was kidding! I'm fine. If I'm hungry I'll go make myself a sandwich."

"I would have gone, you know," she said, sounding relieved.

I looked at her standing there in her old blue pajamas, the ones she wore when Phil didn't spend the night, with cream streaked under her eyes like a football player. "I know you would. Thanks, Mom."

She blew me a kiss. "I'm proud of you, buddy," she said, and closed the door. I took a swig from my water bottle and rubbed my eyes. My mom said she loved me all the time, but proud of me? I couldn't remember hearing that before. It made me sit up and try to figure out what the heck protease was, even though I'd been ready to pass out.

♠ ♣ ♥ ♦

On Monday, the first day of finals, and the day I'd get to see Irina, Mueller asked me to stay after school. Leave it to Mueller to pick the worst day to make me hang around. I thought of how Forrest backed me up in class, and I wondered what kind of devious plan she'd concocted to get revenge.

When I got to Mueller's classroom, she took her time squaring some papers on her desk. With her sleek blond hair and light blue eyes, she would have been pretty if she weren't such a hard-ass. When she finally looked at me, her face was cold. "Hello, Gabriel."

"Hi, Ms. Mueller."

"I'll make this quick. Mr. Newport called a conference with me and several of your other teachers. You're lucky to have him as an advocate." Pause. Stare. "As you know, your grade is in a precarious place right now."

"Yes, ma'am."

"Mr. Newport spoke strongly about your potential and motivation. Unless you get over ninety-five percent on your essay and your multiple choice test, you won't pass this class. So I'd like to offer you the opportunity to earn some points with an additional essay." She looked like she was tasting lemons, forcing the words out her mouth.

"Thank you," I said.

"Five pages, twelve-point font, double-spaced. The topic is . . ." Her lip curled. "What you believe in. What you would fight for. What is that, Gabriel? What gets you motivated? Tell me about it." Her tone said she didn't think there was one damn thing that could motivate my sorry ass.

"Okay," I said.

"You need to study for finals this week, so you may e-mail it to me next Saturday by five p.m.," she said. "And if for some reason you get over ninety-five percent on both your essay and your test,

I'll e-mail you by nine a.m. Saturday to save you the trouble." She sounded like that was about as likely as finding a trillion dollars in my desk.

I nodded and walked out.

♠ ♣ ♥ ♦

By ten thirty p.m. I was showered, dressed, smelling good, pacing, itching for midnight to get there. I had bought something for Irina—found it by accident at our neighbor's yard sale, which was pretty much on our lawn, since we shared a wall.

It was on a blanket with a bunch of jewelry and watches, this cool black painted egg with a sticker that said, "Russian Egg." It had a tiny picture on it of a girl and a bear in a forest. It was hard to believe somebody had painted details that small. It was only two bucks, so I bought it, and now it was in my pocket, and I kept squeezing it like a stress ball and wondering if she'd think it was stupid.

Finally I couldn't stand waiting anymore. I left and drove fast through the empty streets. Redmond was sleepy after eleven, everybody holed up getting rest so they could rule the world better. I couldn't wait to tell Irina what happened with the cop. I'd build it up and let her worry about the ending, then tell her how he let me off.

I parked the car at Angel Point, walked to Irina's house, and sneaked around back. All the windows were dark; that was good. I waited behind one of the trees in her yard. The air felt icy, and the moon was a white sliver above the black roof. Something was dripping.

11:50. 11:51. 11:52.

I swear I looked at my phone every minute. Finally it hit midnight. I kept my eyes on her window. She had the ladder; she'd have to drop it to me.

The window stayed shut.

I stared at the same spot so long, the whole house started to look weird, and I had to blink a few times. I checked my phone. 12:07. *Did she forget?*

Or maybe she didn't want to come out.

I thought about Friday night. Why did I tell her about my dad? Nobody says it, but everybody thinks it: if you come from a screwed-up family, you're damaged goods. Even the trailer trash and gangbangers I hung with in White Center knew who their dads were. I used to tell people my dad was dead, because there was nothing worse than having people think your mom was sexing so many guys, she didn't even know who she had a kid with.

I'd broken one of the only rules my mom taught me: Don't say something important right when you first think of it. Sleep on it.

Oh well. Irina was just a girl, and there were a million girls in the world.

I checked my phone. 12:10.

I should have known she was just like her parents, too good for me. Why did I ever chase her? There were plenty of girls who were into me, like Becky. I should have stuck with that. I hated myself sometimes. I said I'd never let a girl get power over me—I'd seen how it had messed up my friends—and here I'd let it happen.

12:18.

I felt shaky and pissed. Screw her and her whole rich, stuck-up family. I squeezed the egg and wished I could throw it at something. I turned to go and then—I couldn't help myself—I walked back to the side of her house and stared at her window one last time. *Open.*

Right away I hated myself for being weak. I dropped my eyes— and saw a white envelope propped on the window ledge. It had blended into the frame when I was standing farther back. I grabbed it and tore it open.

Gabe,

 My parents caught me climbing in the window the other night. They've got the alarm system on for all the windows and doors, and they're making me sleep in the dressing room attached to their bedroom. I have a concert at Seattle Center on November 7 at seven p.m. in Center House. Meet me by the restrooms at intermission.

Kisses,

Irina

I squeezed the paper, crinkling it. Then I crouched and set the little Russian egg in the corner of the windowsill. Maybe she'd find it and know I'd been there. I dodged away, ran down the sidewalk, and got in my car. November seventh. A little more than a week.

CHAPTER FIFTEEN

Finals were a brand-new version of hell. At my old school, we would complain, get high in the bathrooms, and help each other survive, but at Claremont, people were walking around with books open, like cartoons of nerds. I would have killed to meet just one other screwup, but the Eastside didn't roll like that.

In the afternoon, I had the big science final. When I walked in, most people were already at their desks, silent and clenched up as if they were about to walk the plank. Newport was famous for hard tests. I slung my bag over my chair, sat down, and pulled out my pencil. I was actually sweating.

Newport passed out the exams and we got to business. It was ridiculous how loud everything was: a damn testing soundtrack. The girl behind me breathed like a stalker, and this other guy had a throat-clearing problem that sounded like he was trying to hack up change. The clock was as loud as the timer on *Jeopardy*.

The test had a million tentacles. As soon as I found a question I knew, two more popped up to wrestle with. I got the sick, headachy feeling I always got when I had to read a lot, and the questions wouldn't stay still on the page. But I did my best, and I knew I got some of them right. The sessions with Newport had definitely helped. Still, I was one of the last ones finished, because it took me forever to check the written part to see if I was missing words.

Also, I kept thinking about Irina. I couldn't stand what her parents were doing to us. I wanted to hold her, talk to her, so bad . . . And I was sick of sneaking around. It wasn't supposed to be like this. How long would this go on? Freaking ladders and notes on the side of the house?

When I finally dropped my paper on the pile, Newport looked up from his desk and gave me a kind smile. "I bet you did great, buddy. Good luck on your other tests."

"Thanks, Mr. Newport." I headed for the door. The only thing on my mind was Irina. Just over a week to go.

♠ ♣ ♥ ♦

The rest of the tests weren't as bad. On Wednesday I had the math final, and the studying paid off: there were only a few answers I didn't know, and it was write-in, not bubbles, so that was on my side. On Friday, I messed up the *Hamlet* test pretty good, but I was doing that extra-credit essay, so I figured I'd pass.

I left school Friday afternoon feeling mostly relieved, except for Mueller's extra-credit paper still hanging over my head. I couldn't believe she made it due on Saturday. Who does that? I had plans to go to Forrest's end-of-quarter party that night, and I didn't want to deal with the essay the next morning after no sleep.

The worst part was, I wasn't sure I could find the right essay online for such a specific question. Mueller had a bullshit meter. I thought about asking Missy to help, but there wasn't time for that, so I sat down in my room with my laptop Friday night to see if I could come up with something myself.

I cleared my desk of tempting stuff: my phone, a bag of chips, and even random mail. I scratched at an old Seahawks sticker on my desk . . . and forced myself to look at my computer.

What *did* I believe in? What would I fight for? Of course Mueller had to ask me the hardest question in the universe. It made me depressed, because I started thinking how I actually didn't know what I believed in. My mom never took me to church. I never read any philosophy books.

Fight for? Well, I might fight for Irina, if she needed me, but hell if I was going to say that.

I guess I'd fight if they drafted me.

Shit.

I stared at the screen for a while, but I couldn't concentrate because those fools at Crayola Construction made our town house out of foam core and Elmer's glue, and I could hear Mom and Phil right through the wall. I couldn't exactly make out the words, but the way their voices sounded gave me a pretty good idea of what they were saying.

Blah blah blah . . . I'm whipped and needy.

Blah blah . . . Stop nagging me.

Blah blah blah? . . . When are you leaving her?

Blah blah . . . Stop nagging me.
Blah? . . . When?
Blah blah! . . . Stop nagging me!

I pictured my arm punching through the foam core, grabbing Phil around the neck, and shaking him so hard, his spine snapped. Then I'd get Mom a wonder drug that gave her X-ray vision to see through bullshit. She'd look at Phil and see nothing but a pair of glasses.

I looked at the keyboard. What was I doing? I'd been taking tests all week, and now I was slaving over another piece of writing? Forrest was having a party, and I was sitting at my desk *writing an essay?*

I went to one of the sites that sells term papers, and typed "What do you believe in?" There were hundreds of hits . . . Guess it wasn't such an original question after all. I read a list of titles and picked "I Believe We're All the Same Underneath."

It was a bunch of crap. We're not all the same underneath, and anybody who says so is high. But it seemed like something Mueller would like. I had to doctor it to fit the assignment, but it didn't take long.

As soon as I hit "Send," I bolted out of my seat and dug my stash out of the closet. I bet tonight I could unload a quarter of the stuff at least, and pass along the rest to Kyle. I wanted to get it off my hands.

♠ ♣ ♥ ♦

Forrest had his own entrance, and the bass was shaking the door. I walked into a cloud of smoke and a buffet of California Pizza Kitchen lined up by two pony kegs, thanks to Forrest's parents.

They were the types who wanted to be cool so bad they probably would have catered crack if he had asked them to. The place was packed with people talking and dancing and playing quarters, or just standing in front of the kegs, trying to get trashed before the beer ran out.

Kyle hollered, "Gabe!" and shoved through the crowd to give me a one-armed hug. "We're done, dude! Least for this quarter. Cheers!" He tried to clink glasses, realized I didn't have a drink, and handed me his. "Thisses scotch. My grandpa ordered it twenty years ago, with special oak and stuff. Been cooking for twenty years! You like scotch?"

I downed the glass. "Tastes okay to me."

"That drink you took! Thass like fifty dollars!" Kyle laughed.

"Got any more?"

He held up a finger. "Be right back."

I wandered through the crowd until I found my people: Forrest, some other rowers, and a bunch of fine women. Matt's parents didn't let him go to Forrest's parties, which was probably good because he would have taken one look and left anyway.

Kyle came back soon with a bottle, and we passed it around and talked about—*finals?*

At first I thought I was hearing things. Were these freaks seriously rehashing the test questions at a party? I couldn't believe I'd spent all week being tortured and now had to relive stuff like "Why did Hamlet . . . ?" Did these people know how to have fun?

Even though I thought they were crazy, I couldn't help listening, and I realized: they knew what they were talking about. And their answers were different from mine.

Suddenly I was so pissed, I wanted to punch something, wanted them all to shut up, these smart bastards who knew things about Hamlet that I couldn't figure out if you cut open my head and scanned in the whole play.

I took another swig of scotch, slid the backpack off my shoulder, and dropped it on Forrest's bed. "Open for business," I said.

It was a magnet. People crowded around, digging out cash, talking with their friends about what to buy. One dude actually tried to write me a check. The scotch was potent, and I wasn't thinking straight, or I wouldn't have been doing business in the open like that. But it turned out fine. I unloaded the designer dope right away because people were curious, and then the Oxies and e started disappearing, too.

A hand shoved four bills at me, hundreds, and I looked up to see Forrest's face. Everything was spinning, and I felt hot. He scooped up a bottle of Oxies, didn't even ask how much they were. He knew four hundred was way overpaying.

"I—" My tongue was thick, crowding my mouth.

Forrest looked up, and our eyes held—his weird gray cat eyes— and then he dipped his head and melted away.

The next person pushed cash toward me, and I noticed my hands were shaking. This was wrong, messed up; I hadn't meant to sell to Forrest. But I didn't know what to do. Something. I had to do something.

"Can you take over?" I asked Kyle.

"Sure. Lemme count." He started to count what was left—Kyle was straight business like that—but I waved him away.

"I trust you, man. Just handle it." I took a last swig of scotch and left the room. What if I went after Forrest and asked for the dope back? Told him I made a mistake? I looked around, but I couldn't see him, and the crowd was pulsing as if I were underwater.

I pushed outside for some air. Forrest lived on his own little nature preserve. You couldn't see another building except for his greenhouse, and there were thick pines all around and a deck with two levels. The cold wind felt good, and the smell of the trees made me realize how nasty it had been inside. A group of girls was hanging out on the deck. Every now and then they gave me looks, and laughter cut through the air.

I dropped into a deck chair and ignored them. Things were swirling and unsteady. Where was Forrest?

Then one of the girls broke off and came over. It was Becky. She was wearing a dress about as big as a Band-Aid, with nothing but a ruffle to hold it up. She had to have been freezing. I pulled her onto my lap. She laughed and squirmed, but she didn't get up.

"You look good," I said, nuzzling her neck. "That's a nice dress." She kissed me back, and I started to pull up her skirt. I was so hammered, I didn't care that we had an audience, but she stopped me.

"Let's go in there," she whispered, looking at the greenhouse.

I picked her up and carried her past her giggling girlfriends into Forrest's backyard. *Forrest's forest. Ha.* I set her down, or maybe dropped her, and opened the door. We stumbled into the greenhouse, laughing, and I grabbed her and kissed her. It smelled so good in there, like flowers and rain, and there were ferns falling from pots in the ceiling, tickling my shoulders.

Becky whispered, "Gabe, hold on. I need to ask you something."

I ran my hands down her body. "Huh."

"Do you have a girlfriend?"

"No." I stopped, took my hands off her chest. "Yes." There was a horrible silence as Irina's face zoomed out of the fuzzy back corner of my mind.

"Yeah, it kind of seemed like you were avoiding me at school. And I heard you were still seeing that Russian girl." Becky's voice was flat. She tugged her dress down.

"I'm sorry." I stepped back. "I'm trying not to cheat on her. Shit."

Becky gave me a small smile. "You're not a very good boyfriend, are you?"

"No." I pressed my fists against my eyes, rubbed, and tried to clear my head.

Becky brushed a fern out of her face. "Why do you like her so much?"

"She's . . . Why are we talking about her?"

Becky's eyes were gleaming in the dark. "Because I want to know."

I leaned against the cool glass wall and tipped my head back, looking at a plant with white flowers. "She's different. She's smart and funny. I just like how weird she is. I know it's crazy." My words were coming out thick.

Becky shook her head. "Then be good to her." A second later, the door creaked closed behind her.

I breathed in the rain smell and blinked. There were halos of light around the potted cactus. My thoughts were muddy but definite:

Becky had saved me from my stupid self.

She was a nice girl, and I shouldn't have treated her like I did.

I had to be good; Irina was worth it.

I had been leaning there, thinking, for ten minutes, maybe twenty, when I heard yells and laughter outside really close. I took a breath and pushed out of the greenhouse. The moon was a strange orange color, heavy and ill.

Kyle streaked past, hauling Erin by the arm. He was laughing, trying to rip off his shirt with his free hand. A beer bottle arced in the air like a shining rocket.

Then Forrest flew past me, arms pumping, breathing rough. I almost didn't recognize him, he looked so fierce, like some kind of animal. His body was lit up with that unnatural electricity that turns the skinniest fiend into someone who can lift cars—if the right pill is underneath. He roared something, I couldn't tell what, and threw another bottle in the sky. There was a tinkle of glass.

"Follow the fucking leader!" screamed Forrest. He disappeared into the trees.

I felt hot and sick. I stared after him.

I knew dealing was bad and I did it anyway and . . . now I had this feeling Forrest would have to pay for it. I should be the one paying for my own screwups, but the world doesn't work like that.

I wandered across the lawn, the wet grass soaking my shoes. Shadows were thick on the ground. There was a bubbling sound and I stopped. A pond. Orange bodies flashed through the water. I watched, trying to find a pattern. I wanted there to be a pattern, didn't want them to be just swimming around blind.

I shoved my hand in my pocket and pulled out the cash I'd made earlier. Forrest's bills were on top, the only hundreds in the stack. I clenched the ends and twisted, but they wouldn't rip. My hands weren't working too good. I peeled off the top bill and tore it in half; then I did the rest of them, letting the pieces drop into the pond. They floated on the surface. I kneeled and pushed them to the bottom, and when they floated back up, I put on rocks to weigh them down.

When the money was gone, I wiped my hands on the grass and looked at the sky. I hoped God was real. I hoped he cared about humans and would take care of Forrest. "I'm sorry," I said.

I staggered across the lawn, around the house, to the cars lining the sidewalk. There was my Altima, finally a car I could be proud of.

I touched the hood. Mine.

Blood money.

I got in and put the key in the ignition . . . but some dinosaur part of my brain said, *No. You're too wasted.*

Okay. I could wait a little while. I leaned back in the seat and closed my eyes. Let things go black.

♠ ♣ ♥ ♦

The next morning, I woke up still in my car, feeling like somebody was suctioning my brain through my ears. Even the gray Seattle light hurt my eyes. I stared blankly at the windshield, covered with fat drops of rain—and I groaned as the night came flooding back.

Becky. Forrest. The money I'd ripped up.

Had I really done that? I worked my hand into my pocket. Empty.

I rested my head on the seatback and closed my eyes again. What good had that done? What was I thinking? Trying to be noble or something? But there was nobody around to see.

My stomach, my head, everything felt wrong. Clips of last night drifted through my brain: The dope spread out on Forrest's blanket like a street fair. Becky's eyes when she said, *Be good to her.* Forrest's crazy yell as he ran through the yard. The fish swimming over money. It was like dirt to them; they couldn't eat it or breathe it . . . We couldn't eat it or breathe it, either, but we worshipped the stuff.

Suddenly I got the strangest feeling. All the ragged thoughts in my head floated away, and I went still inside. I waited. I felt something coming. I was sinking into myself, and my edges were matching up, solid and sure.

Something was telling me:

It was good I ripped up the money.

I had done a good thing.

I was finished dealing.

CHAPTER SIXTEEN

We had two days off between quarters, most of which I spent back in White Center playing cards with Mr. Gonzales and Marquis. On Wednesday, when school started up again, I had that hollow amp you get before a big poker game. That night was Irina's concert. But before that, I had three massive finals grades coming in: English, math, and science. I knew I'd done okay on math, because it wasn't a bubble test. If I got at least a B- on the English and science finals, I would pass.

I pictured Irina's face to calm me down. The last week had felt like a year, but soon I'd be holding her. I thought about the part in her hair, because that's what I always saw when she was in my arms. It was so straight, like somebody drew it with a ruler.

I parked in the front lot—I'd been doing that a lot since I got the Altima—and walked past the quad, zoned out. On my way through the door to English, Jamie Elliott whacked me on the shoulder. "You could at least say hi!"

"Oh, sorry, hey." But my eyes were on my desk. Like all the other empty desks, it had an upside-down paper on it. I could almost see the big red stamp on the other side: "Plagiarism." That was a word that all the Claremont teachers made sure we knew very well.

I walked fast to my desk and turned it over. A-.

A-! And I had screwed up some of the spelling on purpose. Relief is sweet even when you don't deserve it. But after a second a devil whispered inside my head, *That paper was a B, maybe a C. She gave you an A- because Newport is pressuring her. You're a charity case. They're all teaming up to help you graduate, even though you're a* loser *and a* fake. I shoved the paper into my backpack and slouched at my desk.

Ms. Mueller gave a speech about how we all did a good job and deserved a break, and she passed out cookies, which was nice of her, except they were crammed with seeds and raisins. Typical Mueller: she could even mess up a cookie. I felt so twitchy and screwed up that I ate three of them anyway. Then she put on a cheesy documentary about Charles Dickens. I looked over to roll my eyes at Forrest—and he wasn't there.

I got a cold feeling as I looked at his chair. Forrest cut plenty, so that was probably it. He just didn't feel like coming to English. Dude could have taught the class himself. Still I texted him under the desk. *WRU@*

I hadn't talked to him since his party.

I checked my phone three times, risking Mueller's wrath, but he never texted back.

My head was going in bad directions. *Oh shit.* I started sweating.

He'd bought a whole bottle of pills.

Four hundred for a whole bottle of pills. I bet he did them all at once. You weren't supposed to do that. What if he overdosed?

I knew a few people who had OD'd. You didn't talk about it, after they were gone. But we all remembered. There was Alyssa in eighth grade. She and her boyfriend, Connor, were doing junk in his dad's garage, and they went to sleep there. When Connor woke up the next morning, Alyssa was blue.

And there was Malik Hernandez. He—

The door opened, and my head whipped around. It was Forrest.

He looked like hell, but it was him. I was so relieved, my breath felt funny.

He slid into his chair and gave me a weak nod—he looked totally thrashed—and set his head on his arms. He was okay. At least for right now.

With dope, you can never say once and for all that somebody is okay.

♠ ♣ ♥ ♦

The second I saw Newport's face, I knew I'd failed. There's nothing more pathetic than when somebody you admire (yeah, I sort of admired him) looks at you like they're so, so sorry for you. He didn't want to break the news, you could tell. In fact, he didn't give us back our tests in class, even though everyone was bugging him about it. He said he wasn't done grading and he'd e-mail grades that night.

I knew he was lying. This was about me, and the fact that I'd failed. He didn't want me to see a big red F without getting to talk to me about it first.

When he kept me after class, I knew for sure. He took off his thick glasses and polished them on his shirt. He looked younger without them. "Gabe, I—"

"I know I failed."

His eyes widened. "What—did you fail on purpose?"

"No. I can just tell from how you're acting."

Newport looked down at his desk and his cheeks got red. "I'm sorry, Gabe. I didn't prepare you well enough. I know you've been trying during our study sessions, and we just didn't . . . I guess I'm confused. You were doing so well. You seemed to know a lot of this stuff, but it just didn't come through on the test. I'm going to—I'm going to let you do a makeup test, though."

You could tell it cost him to say that. He had a "no makeup test" rule. The poor fool. He didn't know a lost cause when it was staring at him like a mug shot.

"Thank you, Mr. Newport. But that's okay."

"Gabe, I really want you to take it. I feel like it's just not fair to dump you in a school this competitive without the right preparation." But you could see his spark had gone out. He was finally getting it that no matter what he did, he couldn't fix me.

He started talking again, about telomeres and DNA strands and a makeup project, but his words fell on my ears, clink clink clink, not connected. My vision was weirdly clear and sharp. I could see the small letters on the human body poster behind him. Smell the whiteboard pens and air freshener and stale coffee. The books were closing in on me, books and papers and things I couldn't handle.

I interrupted him. "You're the best teacher I ever had. Thank you." I hoisted my backpack over my shoulder and walked toward the door.

"Gabe! Don't take this too hard. This was a setback, that's all. I'll e-mail you tonight. We have the rest of the year to work on this, and by the time you take my class in summer school, it'll be cake. Gabe!"

I let the door shut behind me. I was quiet inside, and very focused. I walked down the hall, down the steps, and into the parking lot. I got into my ride and started the engine and drove slowly out of that place, past all the rows of sweet cars and redbrick buildings—all nice containers for people whose brains worked right.

The leather seats and smell of my car told me I wasn't a complete screwup, though; I'd managed to hustle and get myself something. Because that's what life was, right? A big hustle, all of us racing around trying to get the biggest piece of the pie, build our forts, trick them out, load up on diamonds until we were staggering, wondering, *What am I gonna do with all this shit?*

I turned left down Mountebank, past the "Children at Play" sign. If life was a poker game, it was rigged. Some people were born already holding whole stacks of chips in their arms. Some people had the best plays wired into their brains, ready to—ticktock—start making money.

And then there was the rest of us. We had to fight for it, hustle for it, figure out a way to not be forty years old, raising a kid alone, living in a shitty town house bought by some guy who was married to someone else.

I barely noticed the time going by, and it felt like I was home instantly. Walking up to the front door, I wondered how my mom would react. She wanted so badly for me to be the first person in our family to go to college. I'd never planned on going, but it was sort of nice that she thought I could. And maybe in a corner of my brain I had started playing with the idea, because of Irina and Mr. Newport and Kyle and Matt and Forrest.

But now there was no way. I'd have to do summer school to even graduate.

Mom had been talking lately about Seattle U and UW. She'd even watched some Husky football this season, and I remember being confused, but now I thought I got it: she was rooting for the team of the college her kid might go to.

I pushed open the door, and guess what was lying on the bottom step like a snake? Phil's belt. That bastard couldn't wait? It was the worst possible moment, the one minute when I wanted to be with my mom, just the two of us alone in our own house.

I walked upstairs slow and loud as a warning. Mom and Phil were curled up in front of a football game. And then I got it: I was wrong about the Huskies. She wasn't watching them for me. She was watching them for him. Because he liked football.

I took a Coke out of the fridge and walked past them. Phil's face was making me so sick at the moment, I couldn't even say hi to Mom.

"Hi, Gabriel," he said.

Mom clicked the remote and turned off the tube. "Gabe, you want to sit down?"

They knew. Somehow Mom's psychic streak had kicked in (she could always tell when I'd been in a fight), and she knew I'd failed. I frowned. "What?"

"We'd like to chat with you about something," said Phil. He glanced at Mom, and she gave a little nod. He said, "We have some good news for you."

"Phil left his wife," said Mom, and she started to cry.

I stared at them. I was having a hard time breathing.

Phil looked embarrassed. "I, ah, think you're aware that I've been in a troubled marriage, and my only hesitation to commit to you and your mom was out of concern for my . . . ex-wife's mental health. But we've finally . . . ended things."

"He's moving in." Mom's eyes were shining with happiness.

Phil squeezed Mom's shoulder and smiled at me. "Hope that's okay with you."

"No! That's not fucking okay!" *Is that me screaming?*

"Gabriel!" Mom gasped. She stood up, as if that would stop me from saying anything else. "This is a special day for us, and I'd appreciate if you wouldn't ruin it!"

But all I could see was Phil's smug red mug as he leaned back on the couch he bought in the pad he owned, looking at me man-to-man and saying he was moving in. And behind his yellow-ass drinks-too-much eyeballs, there was a cheating, conniving, woman-screwing brain that was always clocking to get laid. I was sure—no, *positive*—that he already had another girl stashed somewhere, because everyone knows that when the player makes a woman his main wifey, she's toast. And I was supposed to live with him, knowing what kind of bastard he was and what my mom was in for?

Phil stood, too, and took Mom's hand like they were a team, and all these things melted into a red bull's-eye of rage on his face.

I punched it as hard as I could.

Phil fell straight back on the couch, his mouth pouring blood.

"Phil! Oh no, honey! He didn't mean to! Gabe!" Mom sounded so horrified, it brought me back to myself. I didn't hit him again, even though I was high on the taste of blood and wanted more.

I made myself walk away. Go upstairs. Slam my door.

Then I started packing. Because even though I was in a rage, my brain was like a blade cutting open the truth: Mom had picked Phil over me. And I was getting the fuck out and never coming back.

I had some nice threads from dealing, and I crammed them in a duffel bag along with a few Gs, which was all I had left after buying my car. I put my kicks in another bag, and dragged all of it, plus my blanket and pillow, downstairs. Phil was sitting on the couch, holding ice to his face. He glared at me as I walked past.

Mom followed me to the front door. She was crying, of course. "Where are you going?"

"I'm moving out."

She made a sound like she didn't believe me.

"'Bye, Mom. Have a nice time living with Phil." I didn't look back, and she didn't come after me. I threw my stuff in the trunk and tore out.

Where was I going? White Center? I had plenty of places to crash there.

But why think small? Why even stay in Washington? There was nothing to hold me here except school. I decided right there. Fuck school. I was dropping out. A dark happiness filled me. She'd be sorry.

But Irina. What about Irina? With that same cold, clear thinking that I'd been having since I walked out of Newport's class, I knew there was no future there. Sooner or later she'd find some tie-wearing douche with a trust fund and marry him.

But then I thought about her tiger eyes. I sort of cared about her. I turned for the I-5. I was going to Winterfest to her concert. I had to at least say good-bye.

♠ ♣ ♥ ♦

Seattle Center was packed. The concession stand lines were twenty, thirty deep; little kids were screaming and running everywhere, and the folding chairs set out for the concert were already filled. A few of the musicians were onstage, tuning their instruments.

There were still twenty minutes left until the concert. My heart was banging in my chest, and I was sweating. Where was Irina? Backstage? I needed her *now*.

I pushed aside the curtain and went in. It was insane, with a skinny Asian guy yelling at everybody, none of them listening, paper music rustling, and everyone talking at the same time.

I felt sick. *What if she isn't here?*

Then I saw her in the back, rubbing her bow on that little block like pool players use.

She looked up and caught her breath. Then she put down her bow and practically ran over. "You were supposed to meet me by the restrooms at intermission!" she whispered. "What are you doing back here?"

"I need to talk to you."

"My dad is here! He knows all these people!"

"Irina, please. I need to talk to you."

She gave me a strange look. "Are you okay? No, never mind. Meet me in a minute by the water fountain. It's in the hall by the restrooms. Can you *go*, please?"

I left and went straight to the fountain. It was quiet back there, a long, empty hall of closed doors. I leaned against one of them and closed my eyes. I was getting an idea. It was a crazy idea, but it was running through me like fire.

A second later, Irina slipped into the hall, looking nervous. She pulled me into the family bathroom, turned the lock, and the light hummed on. It smelled like air freshener, and someone had left the changing table down. It seemed crazy to be standing there with Irina next to a changing table. I gave a laugh that sounded weird to my own ears, sharp and edgy.

Irina hugged me. Just feeling her in my arms made me breathe slower. She said into my shoulder, "Gabe, what's wrong?"

"I'll tell you later." I pulled back so I could look into her eyes. "Run away with me." Damn. I hadn't meant to say it so fast.

"*What?*"

I had to sound calm; I couldn't scare her off. "Something went down. I can't tell you about it right now, but I'm leaving. Remember how we talked about going to Vegas?"

Her brown eyes were huge. "Gabe, you know I can't do that. What happened?"

"I can't tell you right now. I'll explain later. But don't worry, it doesn't involve the police."

She stepped back and searched my face. "That's crazy. You can't ask me to run away."

"Just for a few days," I said, even though I wanted more, way more—I wanted her to run away with me for real. "I have money. I'll keep you safe, we'll just go have fun, I have that ID for you . . ." I tried to slow down. I *was* starting to sound crazy. But I needed her to say yes; I needed to know that there was one woman who had my back, who would take risks for me and be there when I needed her, no matter what.

"Just for a little while," I said again, forcing myself to talk slow. "Please."

She looked really worried. "You're not thinking straight right now."

I took her hands. "I am thinking straight. And I want to have this time where it's just us, doing what we want. Nobody's going to give it to us. We have to take it."

She gave a half smile. "No, they're not going to give it to us."

"You were talking about staying at my house, remember? How is this different?"

She didn't answer.

"You're too perfect. All you do is work. You need to *live*." I pulled her closer and said in a low voice, "I want to be with you. I know we're not going to have sex, that's not what I mean. I'm saying we have something real. You know we do. I never felt like this about a girl before." When the words left my mouth, I knew I meant them.

Her hands tightened around my back, and she looked into my eyes. "Why can't you tell me what happened?"

"I will. It's about my family. It's not a law thing, I swear. I just— I can't."

"You're not ready to talk about it."

"Yeah."

There was a silence. Then she said, "My parents would kill me."

I felt a burst of hope. "What can they do? You're almost old enough to vote. I think you can decide if you want to go away for a couple days." Suddenly I got an idea. I dug in my pocket and pulled out a quarter. "Heads or tails?"

She shook her head. "No. I'm not betting about this."

"Why not?"

"You don't bet about this kind of thing!"

I just looked at her, holding the quarter in my open hand.

She frowned. Her face was hard to read, but she had that fierce look she got sometimes. "Heads," she whispered.

I threw the coin in the air, caught it, slapped it down on my arm. Heads. We looked at each other.

"I had already decided to come," she said, her eyes gleaming. "Just two days, okay?"

I felt weak suddenly, and I almost leaned on the changing table. "Okay."

"Wait for me in the parking lot at intermission. You know the one behind Key Arena?"

"I'll go out there now," I said. "Come when you can."

"This is insane," she said.

I thought I should kiss her, but then I decided, *No, get out before she changes her mind.* There would be time for kissing later.

As I jogged toward the lot, I replayed her voice. *I had already decided to come.* Hell yeah. She was crazy, a real head case—my perfect match.

CHAPTER SEVENTEEN

We drove with all the windows down, and Irina held her hair to the side with one hand and kept her other hand on my leg. We ate up the 90, blasting Tribe, and with every mile that we got farther away from Seattle, I felt Phil and school and the whole mess washing off me. We didn't talk much; I knew Irina was waiting for me to tell her what happened. But I wasn't ready.

Pretty soon it was night, and I focused only on the headlights rolling past, and the road disappearing under us, and the weight of Irina's hand on my leg. I couldn't believe she'd said yes. She had showed up when I needed her. That was so big, I almost couldn't deal with it.

Around Ellensburg, Irina used my phone to send an e-mail to her parents. I don't know what she wrote, except one time she looked up and said, "We're getting home on Saturday, right?"

I said, "Whenever you want," and she went back to writing.

When we hit Yakima city limits, Irina finally asked, "Are you going to tell me what this is about?"

I tried to think how to explain in the fewest words possible. "My mom's boyfriend is moving in."

"Is he . . . ?" You could tell she didn't know how to ask. "Does he hit her or something?"

"No, he's married."

Irina was quiet for a minute. "Well, if he's moving in with your mom, he must be getting a divorce. Right?"

"Probably." I had to force myself to say more, because Irina deserved it. "My mom always gets mixed up with losers. This guy is a complete asshole. He'll cheat on her. He probably already has."

Irina said softly, "And you're mad that he's moving in, so you're running away?"

"Sort of. Neither of them gives a shit where I go, so it's not really running away. But yeah, I need a break."

"What about when we get home? Will you be able to live with him?"

I was quiet, because I was never going home. Maybe I would just buy Irina a plane ticket from Vegas to Seattle, and never set foot in Washington again. But if I told her that, she'd probably want me to turn around right there. Or she'd ask how I was planning to finish school, and I wasn't ready to answer that.

"Gabe?"

"I'll figure it out later. I just need to get away for now."

"I feel like you're not telling me everything," Irina said quietly. "This guy must be really horrible for you to leave like this."

I reached across the gearshift and squeezed her hand. "It's a bad situation. I don't want to think about it anymore. I want to go to Vegas and have fun."

She tipped her head back, and I could see her white teeth as she smiled in the darkness. "I don't really know how to have fun. You'll have to show me."

"Oh, I will." I drove faster.

♠ ♣ ♥ ♦

By four a.m., Irina had fallen asleep. I put up the windows and spread my jacket over her. She was breathing deep enough that it was almost a snore. I wondered how it would be to have a wife and see her every night like this, slobber coming out her mouth, snoring, makeup streaked on her face, but even more beautiful because she was mine.

I pulled into a gas station and got a couple Red Bulls. I had an idea that we would make a straight shot to Vegas, so when Irina woke up, we'd be there with all the lights around us, driving down the Strip, like she was waking up in a dream.

As we crossed the border into Idaho, streaks of purple lit up the horizon, and the outlines of trees started to show. Then it turned the corner into morning. Washington wasn't short on pretty, but Idaho was big and fierce, flexing its mountains like muscles, with trees like teeth in the sky. We drove past Mountain Home and Grand View, and I started to think about stopping right there and taking Irina up into the woods to explore. I mean, the mountains make you a little crazy like that.

We kept going through Bliss and Wendell and Jerome, and in Twin Falls we got on the 93, heading straight south. Driving for so long made me think too much. I was tired, so my head was just running through the same depressing crap: *Nowhere to go. No future. Dropout. Can't even go home.* I wanted to get to Vegas already and blow the thoughts apart with some drinks and games.

Irina finally woke up around ten. Girls are so pretty when they wake up. She stretched like a cat, rubbed her eyes, and said, "Where are we?"

I showed her on my phone, and she couldn't believe we'd come so far. She looked at the empty Red Bull cans in the drink holders, and said, "You must be tired." I didn't say no, because I was starting to see floating dots that I couldn't get rid of no matter how much I rubbed my eyes.

"Let me drive."

I shook my head. "I got it."

"Don't be stubborn. You sleep and I'll drive, and when we get to Vegas, we'll both have energy." She squinted at my phone. "We have *hundreds* of miles to go."

I didn't fight, because I thought I might start hallucinating if I kept going much longer. We took a rest stop, and I switched places with her and let the seat back. "Be careful. The brakes are sensitive."

She smiled. "I'll take good care of your baby." She turned to a classical station, and I'll say one thing for that music: it puts you to sleep.

When I woke up, "Nowhere" was a place, and it was flat and brown, with scrubby plants and rocks and cactuses and short, spiny trees.

The highway didn't seem like it belonged in this place; nothing belonged but coyotes and snakes and maybe outlaws, if they still existed. Off in the distance were red hills with stripes of white and brown and yellow. It was the hardest, emptiest place I had ever seen, and I thought it was even more beautiful than the mountains.

I shielded my eyes. The sun was bouncing off everything in bright flashes. "Are we in Nevada?"

"Yes." Irina sounded proud to have driven all that way. "We're getting close to Ely."

I looked at the clock: Four! We'd been driving—and I'd been sleeping—all day. I straightened in my seat, felt my body waking up. Now that I had some rest, my problems seemed smaller. In my new car, in the middle of the desert with a beautiful girl, going to Vegas! This was how life should be. I rolled down the window, and the air poured in, cool and spicy smelling.

Suddenly I couldn't wait a second longer to kiss Irina.

"Let's stop and walk," I said. "My legs are killing me."

"Good idea." She pulled onto the shoulder, which was nothing but a stretch of red dirt. We got out, and the wind blew more energy into me. It whipped Irina's hair like a flag, and we held hands and walked into the nothingness. Irina was smiling huge. The ground was covered with rocks, sand, and scrawny plants. Big boulders stuck up here and there, streaked with sparkles.

"It feels so good to move!" Irina stretched out her arms.

I pulled her on top of a boulder and kissed her. Our bodies pressed together, and our jackets flapped in the wind. She locked her hands around my neck and pulled me closer. The sun was crazy bright, and the air was cold, and she was kissing me like she couldn't get enough.

I wanted to drink in every part of her. I slid my hands under her shirt, and she pulled back, laughing, and stepped off the boulder. "This place feels like another country," she said.

"I know what you mean." I took her hand and pulled her straight into the desert. We were Adam and Eve on Mars.

"It makes me want to move off the grid."

"Just go off into the wilderness like a hermit or something?" I asked.

"Yeah. Well, not a hermit. I'd want a guy with me." She glanced at me. "My husband and kids, someday. But yeah, sometimes I think about it. I wish I had a big piece of land like this, far away from everything, with no computers, maybe not even a phone, and a beautiful house and a . . . a farm or something. I'd raise my own food."

I smiled. "You obviously don't know much about farming."

"Well, not here, but somewhere you could farm."

"You want to wake up at the crack, squeeze nasty cow titties to get milk, chop wood in the freezing cold, pull a bunch of weeds, and then—what?"

She was giggling. "Did you say 'cow titties'?"

I nodded and said, "Big droopy cow titties," because I loved her laugh. Then I added, "The way to go off the grid is save up bank, rent a cabin somewhere with restaurants like five miles down the road, and live there for a month until you get sick of it."

"That's too easy. I like things to be hard."

"Yeah, you do." I kissed her.

"I warned you." She kicked a stone, and it went thumping across the ground into a prickly bush. "What do you think it was like before computers and cell phones? Before everybody started living online?"

"I bet it was more peaceful," I said. She was actually getting me to imagine moving with her to some shack in the woods.

"Yeah, and more *real*. Like, if people were talking to a person, they were with that person. If they were playing a game, they were moving pieces with their hands. If they were listening to music, it was because someone was right there, playing for them."

I interrupted her. "So you want to go back to before music was recorded? That would mean no—" I almost said Roots, and then I remembered who I was talking to. "No Berlin Philharmonic, unless you went to Berlin."

"I know. I'm not saying I want to live like that. I'm just saying maybe there was something good about the way people used to do things. The Internet and phones just . . . I don't know. They break your brain into a thousand pieces. Maybe your soul, too. Who knows?"

I thought about that. "I'll move off the grid with you for a few months," I told her. "But I'm not farming."

She giggled. "I'll have a vegetable garden, and you can . . . What do you want to do?"

"Stay in the bedroom with you. We can get a patchwork quilt if you want."

She thought that was funny, but I wasn't kidding.

We walked awhile longer, and then she said, "I haven't eaten anything since yesterday. I'm getting really hungry."

I looked at the sun, which was lighting up a million different shades of red in the rocks. "Yeah, we should get back on the road. We can stop somewhere and eat, and then we'll keep going until Vegas. We've got what, three hundred miles?"

"Something like that."

We headed back to the car. Before she got in, Irina bent down, picked up two rocks, and gave me one. It was about as big as a quarter, dark reddish brown, and rough like sandpaper. "So we can remember this place," she said. She tucked hers into her purse, frowned, and moved her hand around under the flap. "Oh yeah. Was this from you?" She pulled out the Russian egg I'd left on her windowsill.

"No, it was from the Russian Easter Bunny."

She laughed and grabbed me and gave me a hard, happy kiss. Then we got in the car and took off down the road.

♠ ♣ ♥ ♦

The first place we saw didn't look like a restaurant, but it had a sign that said "Beer/Food/Lodging," so we stopped. It was a beat-up old shack made of wood so washed-out it looked white, with a tin roof on fire from the setting sun. It was perched on the edge of a hill, and it looked like a puff of wind might blow it down. There was a big deck stretching over the hill on some rickety beams, and the door was open. Johnny Cash was pouring out.

"You sure you're up for this?" I said. "We could find a real restaurant somewhere."

Irina shook her head. "No way. This looks interesting."

I shrugged and followed her up the hill. Long grass was growing between the cracks of the stairs, and burrs grabbed my pant legs. Twenty or so gleaming Harleys were lined up at the side of the building on a long patch of concrete. I wondered how they got up there, and then I saw a dirt road winding behind the place, and I realized we'd come up the back way.

The Cash song ended, and Janis Joplin started belting out "Bobby McGee" in that scratchy, smoky voice of hers. Irina was grinning as she walked through the door. I stepped in behind her and watched every head turn. Fifteen or twenty of the most tatted-up, black-leathered, ratty-bearded, dirtiest muthas I ever saw were crowded up to the bar. There were a couple biker mamas, too, almost as big as their men, with serious cleavage and wicked stares. The place was filled with so much smoke, my first breath felt like taking a drag.

Irina walked right in and sat down at an old Formica two-top. I pulled out a ripped vinyl chair, sat across from her, and looked at the almost-empty squeeze bottle of ketchup, cracked bottle of Tabasco, and rusty silver napkin holder with no napkins left. Mickey's would have to give up the title for Worst Dive.

The bar was a plank of wood against the wall, and it was covered with jars of weird floating things: pickles, eggs, and some scary white blobs. "Feet" was written on the white blob jar in black marker. The ground was full of ashes and peanut shells, and there were old playbills on the wall, and a "Wanted" poster from like a hundred years ago.

"You gonna have to come up here to order," called a high-pitched old man's voice. "I ain't leaving the bar."

"You bring back the menus. I'll save our table," said Irina, grinning.

I gave her a look and headed to the bar. There's nothing like a crowd of four-hundred-pound leathery dudes going silent as you walk up to make you want to turn around and get the hell out.

"You old enough to be in here?" said the bartender. I could see him now, a tiny shriveled guy with a dirty white beard and bright blue eyes. He was wearing a flannel shirt and one of those crazy string ties with a chunk of turquoise on it.

I pulled out my ID and slid it across the bar, but he waved it away. "Just had to ask. What you having?"

"A shot of Jack and . . ." I glanced at Irina. If I asked her, she might say Coke or something, and that was no fun. What did girls like? There was that orange drink my mom used to have. "A tequila sunset," I told the bartender. "Do you have a menu?"

"Nope. We got wings and fries. Which you want?"

"Two of each."

The bartender sloshed my whiskey into a big glass, way more than a shot's worth, and pushed it across the bar. Then he made the tequila sunset with a dirty juice hose and a heavy hand on the tequila.

"Food be out in a minute," he told me. The bikers hadn't said a word the whole time, and it was giving me the willies. I carried our drinks back to the table and sat down.

"What's this?" Irina looked suspiciously at her orange drink. She took a tiny sip and made a horrible face. "It's sweet."

"Sorry. I thought girls liked sweet stuff."

"You could have asked." Irina took my Jack and shoved the tequila sunset in front of me. "Now you have to drink it."

"But—"

"I'm Russian. Russians don't drink cough syrup."

There was a rumble of laughs from the bar, and I realized the bikers had been listening. One of them lifted his beer to me. I grinned at him, then took a sip of tequila sunset. A little cough syrup wouldn't kill me.

Irina frowned. "You're not even going to toast?"

"Oh, sorry. To our trip."

She clinked glasses with me—and knocked back that shot like water. One of the bikers hooted, and I stared at her. She'd pretty much torched my idea of her as an innocent, sheltered girl. "Whoa, Irina! That was a lot of straight whiskey!"

Irina pushed the glass toward the middle of the table. "Russians can drink," she said matter-of-factly. But there was a proud look in her eye, and I had a feeling she was just showing off. The only other time I'd seen her with alcohol, at Morton's party, she'd ditched it on a bookshelf.

"Order up," hollered the bartender. We went to get our food. The wings and fries were piled up in yellow plastic baskets, shining with grease. I slid some cash across the bar and grabbed two of them.

"Why you being antisocial?" one of the bikers said to Irina. "You're supposed to sit at the bar in a place like this." He waved at the bartender. "Two more shots for the lady and her friend."

Irina smiled at the man. "Thank you." She picked up a wing from the basket and leaned on the bar. I set the baskets back down. The tequila was already smoothing me out. I got along with all kinds of people, so why not these guys? The drinks came, and the man clinked his beer against our glasses.

"I'm Beck. And this is T.C., Big Dave, Mad Dave, Butcher, Two-Dog Joe, Spider, Pam, Dino . . ." He rattled off their names, and suddenly there were smiles all around and lots of raised bottles. We'd been adopted by a bunch of Hells Angels.

I slammed my Jack, and after that, things got blurry. I remember inhaling the fries and wings in giant mouthfuls of hot salty grease, and I bought a drink for Beck because he'd gotten those drinks for us. Then I started talking with a skinny guy called

Shingles, who looked part Indian. He had a leather vest and leather pants and a braid of long gray-black hair. Somehow we got into an argument about whether I'd eat a pickled pig's foot, which was what he said the things in the jar were, and I did, and it wasn't half-bad.

Then Shingles said I was all right, between eating the foot and having such a fine woman. I looked around for my "fine woman," and I almost couldn't see her through the black leather. I could hear her laughing, though. Pam and the other two biker mamas were sitting at the bar with their arms folded across their chests, watching the little mob around Irina. Their mouths were running and their eyes were half-shut, the way women's eyes get when they're talking shit.

After a few minutes, Irina broke out of her crowd of fans and came up to me. I didn't like how the men were staring at her, but I guessed I couldn't blame them.

"Can I have the car keys?" she asked.

"Why?"

She gave me a sassy smile. "You'll see."

I shrugged, found the keys in my pocket, and handed them over. She disappeared out the door, and suddenly I wondered why she wanted the keys. She was in no condition to drive, and she wouldn't leave me . . . Would she?

I got up and went to the window. Irina had the trunk open and was pulling out—her violin. I went back to my seat. Should have known she couldn't keep away from it.

When Irina pushed back through the door with her violin, there were mutters from the biker dudes. The bartender turned down the music. He held up his hands and called in his quaky old voice, "Settle down! Settle down!" He had a funny, excited smile, and I got excited, too, thinking how they were all going to be blown away when they heard what she could do on that thing.

Irina stood in the middle of the floor and lifted her violin to her chin. She wasn't holding the bow too steady. It got so quiet you could hear the peanut shells cracking underfoot. Then she closed her eyes and pulled down her bow and *damn*—I don't know what it was, but I'd never heard her play so amazing. It was a fast, wild, lonely tune that seemed perfect for the desert. It showed me a different side of her, a side that wasn't so buttoned down and perfect—the same side that had been chugging drinks for the past hour, I guessed. I heard a tapping behind me, and I turned and saw the bartender watching with his eyes half-closed, his wrinkly hands drumming the counter.

Finally Irina lifted her bow off her violin and looked around the room. She smiled and took a little bow, like they probably trained her to do for concerts. Everybody cheered and hollered—except the women. They looked as if they'd like to take Irina's bow and beat her with it. I clapped hard and whistled.

The bartender said shyly to Irina, "You mind if I have a try? Used to fiddle myself."

She stepped up to the bar and handed over the violin, and the old dude tucked it under his chin and gave us all a mischievous look. Then he pulled the bow down like a gunshot and carved up that violin with the craziest, fastest, gunslinging, devil-down-in-Georgia tune I ever heard. His knuckles were big and red and popping, and his blue eyes were wide-open the whole time. His whole top half was jumping with the music.

When he finished, the bikers roared. The old man was bright red. It was cool to see him so happy. He handed the violin back to Irina.

She was smiling, and maybe even had tears in her eyes, I couldn't tell for sure. "You're amazing!" she said.

"You got a damn fine woman," Shingles said with a sigh. He swept his braid over his back and lit another cigarette.

"You got another one of those?" I asked. I hadn't smoked in a while, but get me drunk enough and I'll smoke lawn clippings if I can't find anything else. Shingles gave me a weird homemade Indian cigarette, and I smoked and sipped on a beer I'd found somewhere.

"Y'all could start a road show," Shingles suggested. "I'll be your manager. We'll travel around, charge people to hear the girl play."

"That's a good idea," I said, wondering why I never thought of it myself.

He squinted and took a long drag. "We'll get her leather pants and a vest, one of them ones with fringe, and a cowboy hat, and we'll do the West. People down there are big on fiddling."

"What do you think we could ask for cover?" I said.

Shingles considered it. "People I'm thinking of ain't too rich. But we could prob'ly get five a head. And if we pack enough of 'em in, we'd make a lot of money."

I started to imagine bags of greasy fives, how fast they could add up, and how much fun we'd have traveling around the country, seeing all the places we'd never been before. I looked around for Irina to tell her—I was thinking she'd like this plan because it was a little like moving off the grid—and I realized she was gone. Her violin was gone, too.

"Well, you'll have to ask the girl if she's up for it, and lemme know." Shingles changed the subject. "I tell you about doing time in Coyote Ridge?" He rolled up his sleeve and showed me a tat of an eagle holding a shield. "That's for my buddy Turo. He flew with the eagles. I met him in Coyote Ridge . . ." Shingles started in on some sketchy prison story, but I was only half paying attention. I was wondering where Irina had gotten to and enjoying the buzz from the Indian cigarette.

In a blurry way, I noticed that one of the biker chicks, the burly blonde, had moved off to the side and was slicking her hair back in a ponytail. She took out her dangly earrings and tucked them in her jeans pocket. Something clicked. I'd seen that before in my old hood—girls greasing up with Vaseline, taking out their hoops, and putting on rings . . .

The woman walked out the back door, moving fast and purposeful. I looked around. Still no Irina. I set down my beer and said, "'Scuse me," to Shingles.

He said, "No, but you didn't say what—" and at that minute, there was a scream. A high-pitched girl scream. Then scuffling and thumping from the back deck, and the sound of glass breaking.

We all ran for the door, and I got knotted up in a clump of leather and sweaty T-shirts.

"Cat fight!" someone yelled. The bikers cheered.

I forced my way through, my pulse hammering. Irina was backed against the wall of the building with those three biker women surrounding her like pit bulls. They were in her face, obviously talking shit, and then the blonde hauled back and slapped her hard.

I lost it. I ran out there, ready to hit a woman for the first time in my life, but one of the men pulled me back. It was like being in a straitjacket, clamped down by his thick leather arms, smelling of tobacco and booze. I bent my head forward and threw it back as hard as I could. There was a crack as my skull hit his jaw. He let go, and I bolted forward just in time to see Irina swing her violin like a bat, fast and hard, at the woman's face.

There was a horrible crunch, and the woman dropped to the ground. The other two backed away as Irina lifted the violin again. She looked crazy, hair blowing back, face flushed, but it was her eyes that were the scariest. They were glittering like she was enjoying herself. She swung the violin at the wall. *Crash.* Jagged pieces of wood dropped to the ground.

The crowd was dead silent.

"No fighting! No fighting on my property!" the bartender's thin voice rang out. He managed to push his way through the crowd, and when he got clear of the bikers and saw Irina standing over the broken violin, he made a strange sound. He knelt down and picked up a piece of broken wood. Then he faced the bikers. His face was red, his blue eyes watery.

"Get the hell off my property! You low-down bunch of hoodlums! Get outta here! Git!" He waved his thin arms, still holding the piece of violin. There were rumbles. Bad looks.

I shook myself as if I was shaking off a spell, crossed the deck to Irina, and put my arms around her. She was trembling, strung tight enough to break.

"Git! Before I call the police!" screamed the bartender.

The bikers slowly wandered off the deck, down the stairs. The woman Irina had hit was clamping a bandana to her eye. We stood there, Irina and the bartender and me, stone still until we heard an engine roar, and the others answer it like thunder. Then the thunder rolled away, down the hill, until it was just a hum, and then emptiness.

CHAPTER EIGHTEEN

The bartender stood looking at the piece of polished wood in his hand. I pulled Irina closer, stroked her hair. Finally he said, not looking at us, "You kids need to rest and clean up. You can have free lodging tonight. I'll get you the keys."

"No, that's okay. We'll be on our way," I said.

He turned and fixed me with an angry blue eye. "Not after all you been drinking. She ain't a violin you can smash up." He disappeared into the bar, and Irina slumped against my chest. She was like a bird in my arms, all heartbeat and bones.

A minute later, the bartender was back with a key hanging off a rope. "Go on. It's over there. I got cleaning up to do." He spit on the deck. He was angry, I could tell. But he still wanted to protect us.

I suddenly felt awful, for messing up his bar, for losing him all that money. I knew none of those guys had paid their tabs. I dug in my pocket, pulled out a couple hundreds, and ran after him into the bar. I laid them on the counter.

"I'm sorry. Thank you for the room."

He looked up from wiping and nodded at me.

I went back to Irina. "Let's stay," I whispered. "We need a break."

She nodded. She was shivering. I put my arm around her and led her to the line of doors in a long, low-down wooden building beyond the bar. I had to lean on the door of our room and push to get it open. I reached for the light. It wasn't much: just a queen bed, a chest of drawers, and a night table with a plastic lamp. The walls were wood boards, and the brown carpet was pretty clean, and it smelled okay. A little musty, maybe.

Irina sat on the end of the bed and set her hands in her lap, turning them over. The dark blue cover was pulled tight across the pillows, and there was an extra blanket folded at the bottom. It looked like the old man took care of the place.

I shut the door behind us and ran some water in the cracked sink, filled a plastic cup, and brought it to Irina. She drank and wiped her hand across her mouth. I sat next to her.

She gave me a sideways look and a tiny grin showed up. "Did you see when I hit the big blond one?"

I nodded. "That was epic."

"They were calling me a slut. The one who slapped me said I was hitting on her man. Can you believe I got her like that? She was way bigger than me." Irina puffed up.

I started chuckling, remembering the other two backing away. Then Irina started laughing, and we laughed until we had to fall back on the bed because the whole thing was so freaking crazy, the only thing to do was laugh. I could tell it was going to go down in history and be one of those things that we brought up again and again, every time we got to reminiscing.

Our laughter finally quieted down until it was just small laughs, and then a giggle here and there. Irina rolled to her side, facing me. Her eyes were gleaming in the almost-dark. She touched my chest.

I kissed her and pulled her into me. She kissed me back, strong and hungry. We rolled back and forth, and she didn't stop me when I lifted her shirt, took off her bra. She was so beautiful, I wanted to explode. She let me touch her everywhere, let me keep going . . . and she didn't stop me when I slid off her jeans.

But she was moving kind of slow. Not totally herself.

She kissed me again—and I could taste the liquor on her breath, as strong as if she'd just taken a drink. I pulled back a little, tried to catch my breath. I felt her hands on my back, moving awkwardly. She was . . . She was drunk. Way more drunk than I was. She had said a lot of times that she was waiting until she was married. She'd meant that.

I rolled away and sat on the edge of the bed.

"What?" she said.

I answered, not looking at her, "You said you're waiting until you're married. I just don't want to do this unless I know it's what you really want." But I was hurting, I wanted her so bad, and I couldn't believe the words coming out of my mouth.

"What I want?" she repeated, sounding mad.

I looked at her and then had to look away again, she was so beautiful naked. "You just did like four shots, Irina."

"Oh, so I have bad breath!"

"It's not that," I said in a strangled voice. "I'm just trying to do right by you. Tell me you want this tomorrow morning, and we will. You're not thinking straight right now. Anyway, people always want to fuck after a fight."

She said in a slurry voice, "They always want to . . . Fine, that's fine. Whatever." I could hear her putting on her clothes.

I stood and walked to the window, leaned against the cold glass. Was I insane? Every one of my friends would tell me I was. I heard the water running in the sink and then the squeak of the bed. I let myself turn around. Irina was lying facedown on the bed, head on her arms.

I sat next to her. She reached for my hand and held it. I stroked her hair. She sighed, and I rubbed her neck, her head, and her shoulders. She started to breathe deeper; then she made a funny gasping sound, and I saw she was asleep.

There was no way to get to the blankets without moving her, so I spread my jacket over her and lay down with my chest to her back, and my chin on her hair. Her breathing was soft and even, and it filled the air with the smell of booze. I closed my eyes and listened to her. Finally my body quieted down, and I fell asleep.

♠ ♣ ♥ ♦

When I woke up the next morning, light was slipping through the shades and falling in bars across Irina's face. She was on her side, and her eyes were open. I squinted and said, "Hey." My head was banging with a slow steady throb. My mouth felt thick and dry.

She kissed my cheek and went to get water. When I'd drunk a glass and propped myself on a pillow, she climbed back on the bed and lay next to me, resting her head on her hand. She looked very serious.

"What?" I said. "Why are you watching me like that?"

"You could have slept with me last night."

I stared at the spiderweb of cracks in the ceiling. It felt weird to be talking about this in the daylight.

"But you didn't, because you said I was drunk and you wanted to make sure it was what I really wanted. I remember."

My face felt hot. "Yeah."

She put her hand in mine. "Look at me." Her gold-brown eyes were wide and serious. "Thank you."

I gave an uncomfortable laugh. "It's fine."

"I didn't realize you were the kind of guy who would do that."

That seemed like a strange, almost mean thing to say. I frowned. "What kind of guy did you think I was?"

"I don't know." She rolled over, pulled a thread on the bed-cover. She looked back at me and pulled the thread again. "I guess I didn't totally trust you."

Now, that *was* messed up. "Then why are you even here with me? You should trust somebody if you're gonna run away to Vegas with them!"

She blushed and tried to backpedal. "That's not how I meant it. It just seemed like you'd been with a lot of girls. I didn't realize you were . . ." She trailed off. "I know who you are now. I respect you. That's all I'm trying to say."

I felt like I was still half-asleep. My head was killing me, and what the hell was she talking about? She didn't respect me before? It was sinking in that she wasn't going to finish what she started last night, either. I wondered why we were even talking about it.

Finally I said, "Whatever. It's not a big deal. I just didn't want your first time to be like that."

She blushed. "I never said I was a virgin. I just said I was waiting until I got married."

"You—what are you talking about? You've had sex before?"

She nodded, looking at the ceiling.

I sat up in bed. I felt shaky. "So that was for nothing?"

She sat up, too. "Are you saying if I'm not a virgin, I don't have the right to decide that I'm waiting? What would you have done if you'd known I *wasn't* a virgin?"

I glared at her. "How many guys have you been with?"

"None of your business, Mr. Can't-Count-His-Partners," she shot back.

"That's different!" I was furious—at her for being such a fake, and at myself for buying it.

She folded her arms across her chest. "How is it different? Did I throw your china statue off a pedestal? Are you allowed to be a slut and it doesn't matter? But if I had sex, I'm *dirty*?"

"No, I'm saying how come them and not me?"

"How hard is it to understand?" she roared, getting off the bed. "It was a mistake! I decided to stop! Haven't you ever made a mistake?"

"When was the last time?" I yelled back. If it was in the past year, I was going to hunt the guy down and kill him.

"That's also none of your business." She walked to the window, opened the slats with her fingers, and looked out. The crack let in a bar of light that showed the pills on the blanket and the dust on everything. I didn't trust myself to say anything else. I watched her thin back and long blond hair and thought, *I always get the raw end of everything.*

Irina said in a low voice, "I lost my virginity when I was fifteen with . . . a guy I was in love with. We broke up last year. That's when I decided to wait until I was married."

"That's kind of extreme!"

Irina shrugged, still looking out the window. "I prayed a lot about it, and I felt like that's what God was telling me." She said in a softer voice, "And I believe that thing about sex joining two souls. It's more than just physical. Everybody acts like it's no big deal. But it is."

"How do you know you won't get drunk again and just screw some random guy who's not going to push you off like I did?" I demanded.

"I don't drink very often," she said. "I just did it last night because it seemed like part of the adventure. But I guess I can't drink around guys at all."

I gave a short laugh. "Yeah, 'cause you're too horny."

She turned and looked at me, her lip curled. "You think waiting is easy? Of course I want to have sex!"

"I don't understand you. How come you like everything to be so hard? If it sucks, you'll pick it," I said bitterly.

"Because doing hard things pays off."

"Fine. Whatever. I'm sure you're right." I pressed my hand against my eyes. "I hope you have a perfect marriage and a perfect life."

There was a long, heavy silence.

"Don't be mad," she said gently.

My anger was slowing down a little. I said, "Maybe this whole trip was you, I don't know, getting back at your parents or something, but it was more than that to me. And I was even okay with not sleeping with you, but it sucks to hear you gave it up to another guy."

"That was before we met, and you don't even know how many girls you've slept with. That's a double standard."

I smashed the pillow, not looking at her. "I know you didn't do anything wrong. I just don't like to think of you with anyone else. You're mine."

Irina walked to the bed and sat down. She picked up my hand. "I like you a lot. But I can't really be yours unless we get married someday, and that's way too far away to talk about."

I looked at her serious brown eyes, her mind ticking away behind them, obviously overthinking everything to the point where she would drive herself crazy, if she hadn't already. I decided this heavy stuff had gone on long enough. We were out here to have fun, and there wasn't much time left.

"I knew you wanted to marry me," I said.

She looked at me in shock. "Shut up."

"You want me to be your love slave."

She giggled. "You'd probably be good at it."

The last of my madness slipped away. I pulled her toward me and kissed the top of her head, her cheeks, and her mouth. "I forgive you for sleeping with that bastard. You just hadn't met me yet. And you *are* mine for right now."

She gave a shriek of laughter. "Well, I forgive *you* for being such a slut! You just hadn't met *me* yet!" We kissed again, fierce makeup kissing. After a while, she pulled back, smoothed her messy hair, and whispered, "See? It's been two months."

"What are you talking about?"

"We're finally getting to know each other."

♠ ♣ ♥ ♦

We hit the road soon after that. It was a little past one, and the bartender was sitting on a plastic lawn chair on his deck, staring at the highway and sipping a Coke from a glass bottle. We had to walk by him to get down the steps to the car. He lifted his hat and squinted at us. He looked washed-out in the sunlight, and very old.

"I left the keys to the room on the bar," I told him. I'd left another hundred, too.

"You want this?" He picked up a paper bag that had been resting in the shade of his chair. The violin handle was sticking out the top.

Irina gave an awkward laugh and said, "Oh no. That's okay. You can throw it out."

He frowned at her. Then he tucked the bag carefully under his chair, leaned back, and pulled his hat down over his eyes.

As I followed Irina down the steps, I said, "What was with the rock-star act, anyway? I can't believe you smashed your violin." I smiled. "It's supposed to be a guitar, you know."

"Well . . ." Irina reached the bottom step and turned around to face me. She shaded her eyes, squinting in the sun. "I think I needed to do it. It was cathartic."

"Yeah, because you practice too much, and you're starting to hate the thing."

She shrugged. "That's true. Sometimes I do hate it."

"But you won't quit?"

She looked horrified. "Just because you hate something doesn't mean you quit."

"Okay, I don't get that." I grabbed her around the waist and carried her, kicking a little, to the car. "But I'm glad you smashed the thing, you badass." I set her down and pretended to swing the violin. "Take that, Philharmonic! Take that, art farts!"

She cracked up. "I think it was more like, take that, Mom and Dad!"

"Yeah, I guess we all do that sometimes." I opened her door for her, and then I slid into the sweet bucket seat on the driver's side—I hoped I never got used to it—and gunned onto the long, empty highway.

CHAPTER NINETEEN

Vegas. Vegas. Vegas.

Even the name is beautiful. To hell with the snobs who think they're above it; Vegas *is* beautiful. It's like a lady dressed up in sequins with tons of makeup on; she doesn't have to be pretty underneath. I loved it the second we drove down the freeway ramp onto Flamingo Road, with giant palm trees lined up on both sides. It was late afternoon, and the sun was lighting up the glass walls of the casinos, and the neon lights were screaming. I loved these crazy muthas who had the balls to build a fake Eiffel Tower and a fake Statue of Liberty and a fake pyramid and a fake Venice and a fake King Arthur's castle. It was like the whole city said, *We're going over the edge.*

"I can't believe we're here," I said to Irina, turning right onto Las Vegas Boulevard.

Her forehead was against the glass. "Wow," she said softly.

I couldn't stop smiling. We drove past Caesars Palace, Harrah's, the Mirage, the Venetian, these big flexing buildings decked out like rock stars. Tourists were everywhere, clutching neon drinks and buckets, like kids going to the playground to dig up treasure. There were skeezy people, and fine women, and way more old people than I would have expected, and packs of guys on the prowl. It was Friday night, and the city was just putting on its shoes, getting ready to make trouble.

I couldn't wait to get in the mix.

I made a right into the Venetian and drove around a long windy road to the valet entrance. The Venetian was a big white Italian castle shooting out of a bright blue lake, with people rowing around in boats that looked like giant elf shoes. A guy about my age in a vest and bow tie came walking over. He opened the door for Irina, handed me a ticket—and we were free.

I grabbed Irina's hand and led her to the sidewalk. The rubber band of excitement in my chest was getting tighter. "Where do you want to go first?"

She looked around, eyes sparkling. "Caesars Palace. I like those commercials."

"Yeah, Caesars seems like classic Vegas."

Walking down the Strip was like being plugged into a giant outlet. Even outside you could hear the machines clinking. A carpet of party flyers was tacked to the ground by too many feet, and billboards flashed pictures of boxing champs and plush suites and snow-white plates of steak and shrimp. Even the Mickey D's was lit up with sprays of lights that kept changing colors.

We crossed the street and hit Caesars through the Forum Shops entrance. It was brighter inside than outside, and for a second I thought it had suddenly turned into a perfect blue-sky, puffy-cloud day just for all the rich shoppers.

Then Irina said in amazement, "It's a fake sky!" I started laughing. Of course it was fake. Everything was awesomely, hilariously fake in this place.

The Forum was packed with shoppers loaded with bags, but off to the right I could see a stretch of dark red carpet and the twinkling gold of handrails. Under the roar of voices was the clang of slots and the click of chips, and under that, I knew there was the whisper of cards.

Somewhere in that room was a spot in front of a Texas Hold'em table.

"You ready to try out your poker skills?" I asked.

Irina gave me a sideways look. "We can't play here. This is for real players."

"I'm a real player," I said, kind of offended. "We could start with the five-dollar tables if you want."

She shook her head.

"Then be my good luck charm." I started pulling her toward the floor—and then I realized how selfish I was being. I stopped. "You want to look around the shops or get a drink or something?"

"I thought you wanted to gamble."

"Nah, this is your vacation. We'll do whatever you want."

Irina slipped an arm around my waist and smiled up at me. "That's sweet, Gabe. No, let's go in there and play for a while."

We hit the floor, and I went to the cage and got some chips, and then followed the signs past the Sports Book to the poker room. Irina was holding my arm, and her grip got pincer-sharp when a

Samoan security guard rolled up. He had a mic clipped to his collar and a bored expression. "Gotta be twenty-one to be in here."

I pulled my card out of my pocket, hoping Irina wouldn't blow it by looking nervous. But she was completely cool as she handed hers over. The bouncer glanced at them, handed them back, and said, "Have a nice time."

I signed in at the desk for no-limit Texas Hold'em, and the hostess took us straight to a table. There were five other players: a young guy in a greasy suit who looked to have been awake for at least a couple days; two women my mom's age checking out every dude who walked past; a tough-looking Mafia type stacking his chips in perfect piles; and a long-bearded old man in a button-down "Jack Daniel's" shirt who looked like he might fall backward any second. His eyes were half-shut, he had his hand wrapped around a beer, and some kind of poker guide was cracked open across his leg.

Irina and I looked at each other and almost started laughing. We were getting to that point where we could read each other's expressions and set each other off. I pulled out a chair for her, but she shook her head and said, "I'll just watch from behind you."

The dealer looked bored enough to shoot himself. He was a frat-boy sort with short blond hair. His uniform had a red bow tie, which I bet he hated. He dealt the hole cards, not even looking at me, although his eyes did run over Irina.

I kept an eye on the other players, already looking for tells. The Mafia guy had at least two thousand in chips, maybe more. But I had a feeling he wouldn't even blink, let alone twitch or do anything helpful. The old man had barely any chips left, and he was so trashed, I didn't think he'd last much longer. He kept cracking ice cubes in his mouth and grinning when people gave him grossed-out looks. The women were staring at the table next to us, probably because a George Clooney look-alike was kicking back behind a monster pile of chips. They were down to one small stack, anyway, so they weren't serious contenders.

Then there was the awake-for-two-days guy. Dude was a picture of the Bad Side of Gambling. He was strung out, scruffy faced, and red-eyed. He needed his mom to give him a bath and put him to bed before he burned up the family fortune, but I had a feeling he'd be up for another three days if he had his way. And his stack of chips said he just might make it.

So it was me versus Mafia Guy and Awake Guy.

Awake Guy posted the small blind, the women (they were gambling together) posted the big blind, and the dealer went to work. I got two jacks, spades and diamonds, and my blood caught fire. Irina smiled, and I shot her a warning glance.

At the flop, Mafia Guy raised us a bill, and the two women folded. Awake Guy glared at Mafia Guy with scary red eyes and shoved a stack of chips in the pot. I could have laughed out loud, because with a jack of hearts, I had a four-of-a-kind on the way, and a good chance of winning that pot.

I raised at the turn, and the old man folded, so it was just Mafia Guy, Awake Guy, and me. Irina was barely breathing. There's something so tight about the last few rounds of a good poker game; it's like chugging a Red Bull. Mafia Guy raised us two hundred; then the last jack showed up on Fifth Street, and Irina's fingers clenched my arm. I almost said, *Ow!* but something like that can be a tell, so I just looked at her. She seriously could have been Awake Guy's sister, stress shooting out of her in wires.

I raised, too. Awake Guy looked as if he wanted to strangle all of us, but he kept up. I started feeling nice and calm, hitting my stride—*oh yeah, they were both going down*—and I could do this for hours.

Time for the showdown. I set down my four of a kind. Mafia Guy sighed and put down a flush. Then Awake Guy giggled and threw down a straight flush!

The old drunk man jerked up in his seat and started to laugh.

I stared at the cards. Bastard had been playing us. I couldn't believe I'd fallen for such a rookie trick. I bet he put soap in his eyes, spilled something on himself, and messed up his hair on purpose.

Well, that was just the first round. Oh, it was on, now.

Awake Guy smiled at me and opened his arms as if he might hug the chips the dealer was raking toward him. I straightened up, got hot. The dealer ran the shuffling machine, and I stared at Awake Guy, daring him to come out of the stocks racing this next round.

Irina pulled on my arm. "Let's go!" she hissed.

"We just got started," I said.

"No, I want to go. Now," she said, way too loud.

Mafia Guy, Awake Guy, and the women stared at us in a lazy, curious way. My face burned. Nothing like being told what to do by your woman in front of a crowd.

"Please," Irina whispered. Her eyes were wide. It hurt to do it, but I scooped up my chips, pushed one toward the dealer, and walked.

As soon as we got away from the table, Irina said, "Thank you."

"Why'd you do that?" I demanded. "That was just the first round."

"Let's get out of here, and I'll explain." A cocktail waitress in a shiny gold dress sliced between us, balancing a loaded tray above her head.

"Well, I'll follow you, since *you're* in charge," I said when we came back together. Irina rolled her eyes, but she turned and pulled me past a row of gold elevators. At the end of the hall was the front lobby with fat red couches and potted trees everywhere.

Irina looked at an empty couch with her eyebrows up. I said, "Fine," and sat down. Stay with a woman awhile, and she starts trying to control you. It happens every time.

I tipped my head back and watched the people swarming by outside on the Strip. Irina sat next to me, but she left some space between us; I'm sure she knew I was pissed. I could still hear the slots in the background.

"I hated that," said Irina.

"I didn't," I said coldly. "That was a good round."

"How can you say it was a good round? You lost four hundred dollars in fifteen minutes!"

"So what? It was exciting."

"It's exciting to lose money?"

I rolled my eyes. "It was tense. There were a lot of good hands."

"That's why I hated it." Irina made a face. "It's like sports—all your biggest emotions, for what? Some cards? Or a football game? Those feelings should be for *war*. I wanted to kill that guy. I seriously couldn't handle sitting next to him one second longer."

So that was it. I poked her leg. "You're too competitive. That's the problem. You can't stand to lose anything, even a couple dollars."

"Four hundred is not 'a couple,'" said Irina. "I just read this book by Chekhov, and he said gambling mocks the sweat of honest workers. I think he's right."

I pulled her into my shoulder. "Come on, you salty woman. Calm down. We won't gamble anymore, since you can't handle it."

Irina leaned into me. Her hand found mine. We sat there for a while, watching the people march, stagger, and wander by outside on the Strip, and the lights flash, and the cars stop and go, with people hanging out the tops and sides, soaking up the crazy air.

Irina said in a low voice, "Gabe, you know how you said nobody would give us this time; we had to take it?"

I looked down at her. "Yeah?"

"It's going too fast. I said I'd be home Saturday. We should . . . I'm scared we'll waste it."

"What do you mean?"

She put her chin on my shoulder. "I mean, it's too easy to get sucked into this place. You could start gambling and wake up a hundred years later, like in that one fairy tale. I don't want to get distracted. I want to get in your head. Like really get to know you."

"You missed your chance this morning," I said softly. I looked into her eyes and realized she was really into me. I could feel it pouring out of her.

She sighed.

"You're going to conservatory, anyway," I said. "Who cares how well you know me?"

"*I* do. And anyway, maybe I'm not going to conservatory. Maybe I don't want to play for an orchestra."

I frowned as the words sank in.

"I've been thinking, what if I went to a regular college? What if I make the violin something I do for fun? I want it to be fun again." She paused. "I don't know. Anyway, I'm not the only one going away. You're going to college. But we have right now. And who knows . . ." She trailed off, looking shy.

College. I was a piece of junk for letting her believe I was going somewhere with my life. She'd find out the truth soon, and we'd be done, but at least I could show her a good time for now.

I brushed her hair out of the way and kissed her forehead. "Okay, we won't waste time. We've been sitting too long. We're in Vegas." I stood and grabbed her hand, steered her out the brass doors and onto the sidewalk. The air was thin and cool.

Irina tipped her head back like she was drinking in the sky. "It feels good out here."

I pointed down the Strip. "Check it out. I think that's the Bellagio." Huge jets of water were shooting into the sky from some kind of hotel pool. A crowd was pressed up against a rope, watching.

We walked over. Classical music was playing, and the water jumped on every high note. A guy dressed like a pirate walked by, showing off his tanned pecs and eighties rock-star hair. He winked at Irina.

She giggled and hid her face in my shoulder. We leaned against the rope, holding hands and watching the water roaring and flying.

Irina said, "Gabe, why are we here?"

I glanced at her. "We don't have to watch this. I just thought you would like it."

"No, I mean, why are we in Vegas? I've been thinking about what you said about your mom and that guy, and I feel like . . . I don't know. I feel like you're not telling me everything. Did something seriously bad happen?" She squinted at me. She was good at letting the silence build until I had to say something.

A giant jet of water finished the show, and the crowd clapped.

I shrugged. The words were stuck in my mouth. I wanted so badly to tell her about failing school, because she'd have to find out eventually.

"No," I said. I changed the subject. "So did you hear back from your parents?" She'd used my phone enough times to e-mail them.

Irina stared into the pool. "Well, they e-mailed eight times, last time I checked. One of them was like three pages. Good thing my dad ruined my phone, so he can't look up your number."

"Why didn't you tell me?"

"I didn't want to mess up our time. Anyway, I don't care. I told them I'll be home Saturday." She tugged my hand. "Come on. Let's go. I want to see everything there is to see in this entire place."

CHAPTER TWENTY

After wandering through casinos for hours, I was feeling kind of dizzy, like I needed a break from the lights and noise. We had played a few arcade games, almost got in a fight with some jerks who were saying pervy things to Irina, and got kicked out of Cleopatra's Barge for PDA.

Now we were outside again, and the Strip was in full swing, screaming with party energy. I should have felt good, but I kept thinking how this was all going to end. Irina had gotten in my head with the talk about not wasting time. I wanted to memorize her, memorize every second, because life doesn't give do-overs. Sometimes people are only there for a little while, and you have to soak them up while you can.

"Let's go this way. I want to see what Vegas is like away from the Strip." We'd just hit a stoplight, and Irina pointed north up Flamingo Road.

"I think it's wannabe Strip," I said, but I turned. The casinos were all starting to look the same, and I kind of liked the idea of just going until we hit the "real" Vegas, whatever that was. We passed the Rio Hotel, a bunch of fast-food joints, a car lot, and a few warehouses. The businesses were getting farther apart, and I started to wonder why we thought this was a good idea.

"What's that place?" Irina pointed to a lit building set back from the road. It was a big log house with a gravel path through a cactus garden, and metal lanterns lighting the doorway.

"Charleston Saloon," I said, reading the wooden sign over the door.

"Do you want to check it out? I'm seriously going to faint from hunger." Irina pressed a hand over her flat stomach and gave me a pathetic look.

"Sure." I scanned the parking lot. It was about half-full of mostly newer cars, plus a handful of high-end rides, like a Jag and a Benz. We headed up the gravel path and through the big swinging door.

Inside, the place was pretty cool: a horseshoe bar, those metal lanterns with holes in them, and Indian rugs on the walls. The smell of food hit me in a wave, and I suddenly realized how starving I was, and thirsty, too.

The hostess was a curvy chick with long black hair, wearing a little white dress and killer heels. It seemed like girls had to be hot to find work in this town. "There's a wait for a table, but I can seat you at the bar," she told us. "Is that okay?"

"Yes," we said at the same time.

She looked closer at Irina. "You're both twenty-one?"

"Yeah," I said. "And I'm sure the bartender will card us, anyway."

She waved us in. "Seat yourselves."

We grabbed seats at the bar, nice padded leather stools, and opened our menus. The bartender, a Mexican guy, set waters in front of us. Out of the corner of my eye, I saw Irina check him out. He was a good-looking dude: shiny black hair combed back, strong build, and that crafty Latin look, like he knew exactly what to say to women—which I'm sure he did. He was tall, too. I looked back at Irina, but she was staring past his shoulder now.

"I bet he'd go out with you if you asked," I whispered in her ear. She shoved me.

"I'll need to see IDs," the bartender said. We showed him our cards. He took a look and handed them back. "What can I get you to drink?"

I'd had enough the night before to last me about a week. "O'Doul's, please," I said. It was what my mom drank when she was trying not to drink. Irina ordered lemonade, and before the bartender could walk away, I waved the plastic happy-hour menu and said, "Can we get one of everything?"

"Sure." He went to the island and brought back a bowl of chips and some salsa. "Sounds like you're hungry. This'll get you started."

We started inhaling chips and got into one of those conversations where we replayed everything we'd seen that night, talked trash, and tried to figure out what we really thought about Vegas. I ate with my left hand so I could hold hands with Irina under the bar.

Finally the food showed up: wings, nachos, cheese fries, mozzarella sticks, and these nasty fried oysters that we never should've ordered, except we were too hungry to know better. Eating made me less shaky, but underneath, there was still the feeling that the clock was ticking. It was Friday night, and tomorrow Irina would be back in her normal life, and I would be . . . fucked.

The bar was starting to fill up, and a pack of people took the line of seats next to Irina, talking to each other in some hacking language. They sounded like the bad guys in a lot of movies, and I was pretty sure they were Russian.

"It's your homeboys," I whispered to Irina.

She was smiling. She said something to the girl sitting next to her, and the girl squealed and said something back. Pretty soon everybody was yacking in Russian. For about a minute it was sexy to hear Irina talking in another language; then I got bored. But I decided it was good she was taken care of because I had to think about some things, like deciding what the hell I was going to do next.

I would buy Irina a plane ticket back to Seattle; that much I knew. But then what? After the ticket, I'd be down to about three grand, which could last me a little while if I was careful, but then again, I wasn't that good at being careful.

I needed money. A place to live. A plan.

Maybe I'd just keep driving and see as much of the country as I could until my cash burned out, and then I'd get a job wherever I landed. I'd have to stick to the coasts; I didn't want to wind up in some one-pump town.

I watched the bartender doing his rounds. He never hurried, but somehow nobody had to signal him; he was right there whenever a drink was empty. It started to look like magic after a while. I wondered how he kept his shirt so white even though he lived around Coke and cherries. And he was sweeping up official cash: fives and tens and even twenties.

That was the great thing about Vegas. Normal people like card dealers, valets, and waiters could tap into the money coming into the city. The tourists were the heart that pumped money through the body, and yeah, the big cash was for the big boys, but the money flowed to the fingers and toes, too, the working parts.

I watched two women flirting with the bartender, tipping him a twenty, and I imagined me back there, chatting with people, sweeping up cash, fixing drinks.

Why not? Girls thought I looked good. And I'd like to talk with different people all day, give them a little happy-juice when they needed it, listen to their problems or their good news.

Next time the bartender swung around to see if we needed anything, I asked for another O'Doul's and said, "Bartending must be a sweet job, huh?"

"Yeah, it's got a lot of benefits." He glanced down the bar.

I thought he was talking about the women, so I said, "No doubt. All the hotties are hitting on you."

He laughed in a nice way. "Maybe so. But I got enough women to handle already, you wouldn't believe."

"Yeah, it seems like women need a fine card to get into this city or something."

He turned and grabbed something off the register a few feet behind him. "No, man, this is what I'm talking about." He showed me a picture in a plastic frame, of him and this Mexican woman and—*whoa*—five little girls! His face was almost crowded out of the picture from a baby he was holding, and the other ones were squeezed between his shoulders, grinning at the camera. His wife was wearing a pink shirt, and she had a big smile. She looked nice.

"You got a beautiful family," I said.

"Thank you." He took the picture and put it back on the register carefully. If I ever had a family, I hoped I would be like that with their picture.

"So, how long have you been bartending?" I asked.

"Ten years, since I got married and we moved out here. Great money, and you don't have to take work home. It's a good way to support a family. But you're probably not thinking about that yet." He glanced at Irina, who was still chatting with her new friends.

"I don't know. Maybe I am," I heard myself say.

His eyebrows went up. "Well, it's a good job. But you have to know how to handle drunks, how to stop fights. And you have to make great drinks. But you also have to know when to cut people off."

"Huh," I said. "So where does somebody learn how to bartend?"

He scanned the bar again, checking if anybody needed him. "Depends what kind of bartending you want to do. There's the show-off stuff in nightclubs, juggling bottles. For that you go to Flair School. But if you decide you want to do real bartending, go to Crescent School, then find a job somewhere local, not the Strip."

"Why?"

"You get regulars in a place like this. You make friends, and you get better tips." He evened out a stack of napkins. "But the Strip is okay, too, if you like excitement. Just handle your bar like a man, and you'll be okay."

I wanted to ask him what that meant, *to handle your bar like a man*, but I was afraid I'd sound like a weirdo. "So where's Crescent School?" I asked.

"On Sandhill. Listen, it's none of my business, but"—he glanced at my O'Doul's—"bartending isn't the best job if you're trying to avoid liquor."

I looked at my bottle and started laughing. "Oh, man, no, I don't have a drinking problem. I just felt like O'Doul's."

He smiled. "That's good. If you can take or leave liquor, you'd be a good bartender."

"Yeah, that's me," I said. "I like it, but I never need it or anything."

"You like people? You like to talk a lot?"

"Yeah."

"You stay cool in a fight?"

"Mostly."

"You willing to be on your feet all day?"

"Yeah!"

"You not afraid of some grunt work, like dishes?"

"No."

"You keep yourself looking nice, keep your hair combed . . . Never mind. I see you got that handled." Just then, somebody held up an empty, and he disappeared.

Irina turned to me. "Gabe, this is Marina, Yuri, Sasha, and Katya." I lifted a hand, and they nodded at me or said hey. What is it with Russian dudes being twice the size of American guys? They were dressed up nice, in sports coats. One of them looked like a younger version of Irina's dad.

Suddenly I realized I didn't have that much time left with Irina, and I sure didn't want to waste it not talking to her. "You want to bolt?" I said in her ear.

She nodded. "Give me a second."

I put out some cash to settle up, and the bartender's magic sensors brought him around to grab it. He gave me change, and I slid him a twenty for a tip. "Thanks for the advice, man. I'm going to do it," I said.

"You'll like it. It's good work." He paused, looking me over. "Listen, you're going to have to start with bussing or barbacking. Economy's not so hot right now. Nobody gets a bartending gig right away in this town."

"Yeah, I'm okay with that." I didn't know what a barback was, but I would do it.

"You a hard worker?"

I hoped he was going where I thought he was going. "Yeah."

"I'll ask around, see if anybody needs a busser or barback. All of us bartenders know each other. Come back and see me in a week. I'll tell you if I heard of anything."

It was a sign. "Thanks, man!" I was smiling huge. I didn't care that Irina had turned away from her friends and was staring at me as if I'd changed color.

He nodded. "Sure thing. Have a good night." Then he was gone.

"What was that about?" Irina said.

"I'll tell you in a second." I glanced at her friends. She waved good-bye, and we headed out the door into the cool night. The desert sky was black past the casino lights, and the stars were popping. I was stone sober and felt better than I had in about ten years. I wanted to holler into the air.

Irina looked worried. "It sounded like that bartender was offering to help you find a job."

"Yep," I said, grinning and still looking up. I sent out a silent thank-you in case God was real and listening.

Irina stopped on the edge of the parking lot and faced me. "Gabe, what's going on?"

"Let's sit down for a second." I pulled her onto the curb behind a dark line of bumpers. Her eyes reflected the lights from the restaurant, and she wrapped her arms around her knees and sat very still, waiting. It was time to come clean.

I wasn't sure where to start, so I blurted out, "I'm not going to be a doctor."

"Okay, I knew that. But you're not answering my question."

"What do you mean, you knew that?" I was kind of insulted.

"A lot of people think they're going to be doctors, and most of them never end up doing it. And no offense, but you didn't seem that into medical stuff. But what about this job thing? What were you guys talking about?"

I put my elbows on my knees. It was hard to get the words out after all this time keeping them back. I said fast, in a low voice, "I dropped out of school on Wednesday. I'm staying in Vegas. Don't worry, I'll get you a plane ticket home tomorrow."

She gasped. "You dropped out?"

"I was failing a bunch of classes." I gave her a sideways look. "I'm fucking stupid, actually." I couldn't believe I was finally admitting it.

"No, you're not!"

Suddenly I needed her to know. "Yes, I am. I can't even read right, Irina. I can't study. My brain doesn't work like other people's."

"What are you talking about? You can't read right?"

"I just can't."

She stared at me like she wanted more, so I tried. "The words smash together, and the letters get all weird. They crawl off the page sometimes. I get sick, like kind of dizzy. It takes me forever to get through a page."

She was quiet for a moment. Then she asked, "Do you have dyslexia?"

I shook my head. "It's not that. That's where you write letters backward."

"Anya's little brother has dyslexia, and he doesn't write letters backward. He just has a hard time reading. And he always says it makes him feel sick. You're smart, Gabe. I know you are. You should get tested. It might be some other kind of disability. Words crawling off the page isn't normal."

The word *disability* made me feel so spooked that I wanted to stay as far away from it as I could. "Who cares what it is? I can't change it."

She stared at me. "Well, you can't just drop out! That would be wasting all the time you already put in. Can't you take those classes over?"

"I'd have to do summer school, and I'm not doing that. Anyway, who says I'd pass them if I tried again?"

"Gabe, you really need to get tested. They have to help you, and give you extra time on tests . . ." Irina trailed off as she saw my face. I was getting pissed, because I felt like she wasn't listening, and I didn't like her saying I had a disability.

"I'm not going back to school," I said as strongly as I could. I wasn't in the mood to argue about it.

After a minute Irina said in a strange voice, "What about your GED?"

"I guess I'll do that sometime, just so I have it. But now I figured out what I want to do, and I don't need a degree for it."

"You're going to stay in Vegas and *bartend*?" Irina scooted down the curb a few inches so she could see me. "But you're not even eighteen yet."

I shrugged. "I have a real ID that says I'm twenty-two. The feds aren't sitting there, matching up birthdays with jobs. Besides, I have to go to bartending school and do bussing or barbacking or whatever. That'll take some time."

"So . . . you're just going to stay here? You're not even coming home?"

"I don't have a home." I looked away. "And besides, you're going to college or wherever. You want me to come back to Washington just so I can say good-bye to you in a few months?"

"I guess not," Irina said softly. She folded her arms over her knees and rested her head on them. After a minute, she said in a low voice, "Well, you'll be a great bartender."

"I know." I threw a pebble at the curb.

"Why didn't you tell me you were having a hard time in school?"

I gave a short laugh. "Are you kidding? Look at you. You wouldn't date a loser."

She put her cool hand on mine. "Don't call yourself that. First of all, I obviously didn't go the traditional school route myself. Second of all, I don't care about money. I don't want to live like my parents. My dad kills himself working, and it's never enough, and all he's buying anyway is a big empty house for my mom to sit in by herself. I don't want that."

She sounded so strong that I looked at her in surprise. I guessed there was still a lot we didn't know about each other. "So marry a bartender," I said, because the talk was getting too intense, and we both needed to lighten up.

She smiled. "Is that a proposal?"

"No. If it was a proposal, I'd have a giant rock and be like this." I dropped off the curb onto my knees, grabbed her arm, and started kissing her wrist. Irina shrieked and tried to get away, and I said in a Russian accent, "Say you vill marry me!"

Just then some people walked out. They looked at us like we were lunatics. I thought I'd give them a show, so I pulled Irina in and kissed her, and it turned into a real kiss, one that lasted way after their car pulled away. Irina slid her hands under my coat and whispered something in my ear that made me blush, which is hard to do.

"There is no way," I said, "that you're going to make it until you're married."

"Oh yes, I am," she said, her eyes gleaming in the dark. Then she got to her feet, and I did, too, and we walked into the night, swinging our hands between us.

CHAPTER TWENTY-ONE

rina and I didn't sleep that night. She checked Orbitz on my phone, and the only flight the next day that wasn't like seven hundred bucks was at six thirty a.m. So we wandered around the streets of Vegas, and we lay in the grass, kissing and talking in front of an apartment building. When somebody yelled at us, we walked some more and found another building and did it again. We talked about stupid things and funny things and deep things. There was a magic feeling, as if we'd knocked down whatever last guard we had up.

We finally made it back to the Venetian around four thirty a.m., and I drove Irina to McCarran International. We parked in the giant garage, and I walked her to ticketing. Even in the airport this early in the morning, the slots were clinking. We went past a bank of machines, filled with people who couldn't wait to lose another few bucks before they got on the plane home.

When we got to the counter, Irina pulled out her credit card, but I pushed it away and made the United guy take my money. No way was I letting her buy her own ticket. I'd gotten her into this, and I'd get her home.

The man printed out the boarding pass, and as we walked away, Irina said in a kind of crazy voice, "Thank you." I looked over in surprise. Was she crying? Her eyes were shiny, anyway. "You're a gentleman," she said, not looking at me.

I started feeling a little weird myself. "Yeah, I'm a real prince."

We were almost to the security line, where we'd have to say good-bye. Irina pulled me out of the flow of traffic, against the wall. She said in a low, strong voice, "You'd better call me every day."

I smiled at her. "You'll have to give me your number."

"Give me a week, and I'll have a new phone." She squeezed my hands. "Gabe." She sounded intense. "I'm crazy about you."

Part of my brain was right there in the moment, but a tiny corner was watching, amazed, thinking, *You love this girl. You actually love her.*

"I'll call every day," I promised. I pulled her into my chest and said in her ear, "Here's what's going to happen. I'm going to learn how to bartend, and you're going to college, and then you'll get a job *not* playing the violin, and I'll come bartend in that city on the day shift, so we can have nights together."

I paused, and decided what the hell. "And we can get married if you want, because I can't do this waiting thing."

"If *I* want?"

"Well, I'd be okay with it."

Irina pulled back and gave me a hard-to-read look. Her eyes were catching the sun, showing flecks of gold. She whispered, "What you said about going to Vegas came true. Maybe this will, too." Then she stood on tiptoes to kiss me.

I guess we made a scene. After a few minutes, I heard someone say, "Get a room," and then I heard the fast clicking sound that they must program into shoes for cops and security guards. I pulled back and yep, a three-hundred-pound guy in a tight suit was giving me the evil eye.

"Call me when you get there," I said.

"I will." Irina gave me a last kiss and hurried into the line.

I wanted to run after her and beg her to stay, to forget college. I'd find a way to take care of her . . . but I knew she'd never say yes, and if she did, she wouldn't be Irina. So I watched her blond hair disappear through the metal detector, and I saw her turn and wave one last time. I waved back, even though I knew she probably couldn't see me.

♠ ♣ ♥ ♦

After paying a rip-off ten bucks, I got my car out of the garage and drove out of McCarran down Las Vegas Boulevard. I passed the famous sign, "Welcome to Fabulous Las Vegas, Nevada." The seat next to me felt very empty. I was strung out in that way you get after a night of no sleep. The Strip looked different in the daylight, with dazed people wandering out of casinos and club flyers fluttering on the sidewalks like confetti from a party the night before.

I looked up Crescent School on my phone, and it was open nine to nine, seven days a week. Typical Vegas. I mapped it, took a right on Flamingo, and drove down a few miles to Sandhill Drive.

I parked in the corner of the lot under some palm trees. The school was in the middle of an office park, a two-story brick building, tired-looking but clean, with cactuses planted around the entrance. Doors were closed, shades down.

I let my seat back and watched as the sky turned brighter until it was an unreal shade of blue. When it got too bright, I shut my eyes and thought of Irina. In the airport she said she was crazy about me, and she *sounded* crazy when she said it. I replayed the words over and over and wondered when I would get to see her again.

♠ ♣ ♥ ♦

When I woke up, my neck hurt and the light was fierce. Compared to Seattle, Vegas felt like the whole ozone layer had been stripped away. I checked my phone: noon! I rubbed my eyes and squinted into the mirror. I was looking torn up, but nothing a shave wouldn't fix. I got my kit out of the trunk, did a quick shave on the down low, and changed my shirt. There was about an inch left of two-day-old Red Bull, and I chugged it.

Then I headed into Crescent School. I was glad to see the inside wasn't too sketchy. The carpet was decent, there was real furniture, and there were framed pictures on the walls of bartenders shaking mixers and sticking fruit in drinks.

At the reception desk was a black woman, seriously curvy, with bright red braids, wearing a suit that was bursting at the buttons. She was flipping through a magazine. Behind her was a row of closed doors. I could hear people laughing and talking back there.

She lowered her magazine and looked me up and down. "Help you?"

"I just wanted to find out more about your school."

She rattled off, "We're one of the only accredited bartending schools in the United States. Training in our simulated cocktail lounge will help you increase your speed, coordination, and confidence behind the bar. You'll graduate in four weeks with a full understanding of liquors and liqueurs, lingo, and customer service tips, the back bar and under bar, bar tools and equipment, and over two hundred cocktails, including the latest shooters. New classes start every second Monday."

She leaned back in her chair and folded her arms. Her eyelids were glittery purple.

"How much does it cost?"

"Nine hundred fifty for the full course. Three hundred for a refresher."

That was a big chunk of what I had left, but it was about what I'd expected. "Yeah, okay." I pulled out my clip, and her eyes got wide.

"What you doing? You just gonna pay cash like that?"

I lowered my hand. "Well, yeah."

"You don't want to see the facilities or nothing?"

Feeling like an idiot, I stuck my money back in my pocket. "Yeah, show me the facilities."

She gave me a look like I wasn't fooling anybody, and stood up. She swished over to one of the doors and held it open. "Come on, then."

I followed her through. When they said simulated cocktail lounge, they weren't kidding. The place was more than just a bar; it was a whole setup. People were sitting at the bar, some more were at tables, and two bartenders were making drinks. The only thing missing was music.

When we walked in, everybody looked up. "Hey, Danitra," called a guy sitting at one of the tables.

"That's Paul, the owner," Danitra said in a low voice. She walked me over. "Paul, this gentleman's thinking about signing up."

Paul was a skinny dude with a brown ponytail, wearing jeans and a "Palms" T-shirt. He stood up and shook my hand, asked my name. Then he said, "Why don't you go to the bar and order something? You can watch them practice." He winked and added, "Make it hard, not a well drink."

I smiled. I liked his vibe—something about him reminded me of Missy, even though he was a guy. I headed to the bar where a man and a woman were mixing drinks. They were both wearing black aprons that said "Crescent School of Bartending and Gaming." There was a line of red stools at the bar, four of them filled. I sat on the empty one.

"Paul told you to order something?" said the guy behind the bar. He looked like he just turned twenty-one, with curly red hair and skin that was blinding white under the lights. I nodded, and he said, "Okay, what are you having?"

I thought about it. What was the weirdest drink I knew? "Chocolate snakebite."

He scowled and threw a quick glance in Paul's direction. "Aw, man. What kind of chick drink is that? Ask for a Jack and Coke or something."

The woman bartender's eyebrows went up. She was Mexican or Spanish, very short and round, with long black hair and a sassy look. "I'll make it."

The guy rolled his eyes at her. "Shut up, Luce. You don't know what it is, either."

"I don't?" She grabbed the Bailey's, Kahlua, crème de cacao, and Goldschläger, and started dumping shots in a metal mixer. I actually had no idea what was in a chocolate snakebite; it was just something I'd heard my mom order a few times, and I thought it was a funny name.

"Is that it?" the guy demanded, looking at me.

I nodded. "She got it right."

Luce gave me a nice smile, shook up the drink, whipped out a glass from under the bar, and poured the shot. She pushed it in front of me. "You don't know for sure until you try it."

I looked at the brown stuff. It was probably sweet swill, but I should at least do her the respect of tasting it. I lifted it and took a good swig—and almost hacked out my tongue. *Nasty!* It was moldy, metal sewer water!

Everybody at the bar, including both bartenders, were about pissing themselves.

"You think they let us practice with real liquor?" gasped Luce. "It's water with food coloring!" Behind us, Danitra and Paul were cracking up, too.

I wiped my mouth and chuckled. "Okay, that was good. You got me." I shook my head. "You got me good." Somebody cheered and one of the people at the bar, a big bald dude, gave me a thumbs-up.

"That was a test," the redheaded bartender explained. "If you got mad, we wouldn't have let you join the school."

"*Really?*"

He laughed. "No, man, we don't get to decide. I'm sure Paul would have taken your money. But we would have spread the word that you were an idiot. But you're in now. You passed the test." He held out his hand. "I'm Aidan, by the way."

I laughed as I shook his hand. "Nice test. I could see some people getting mad."

"Only the assholes," said Aidan, grinning.

After that we had fun; I hung around for a while, chatting with people, watching them practice. They took turns at the bar, and the rest played customers, pretending to be high-maintenance or psycho or just plain stupid. They had different personalities worked out, like somebody said, "Oh, Greg, do the perv!" and this older guy ordered a blow job from a girl bartender and started talking dirty so she could practice how to deal with pervs.

Then this cute brunette said, "I'm Wynn's wife," and kept turning drinks back in and saying, "Only pass the vermouth over the martini, only pass it." The whole thing was like a comedy show where you actually learned something, and I knew after the first five minutes that I had found my spot.

When we went back to reception, I took out my cash again. "Okay, Danitra, sign me up."

She said approvingly, "That's right, honey. You fit right in. You just fill out these forms, and we'll get you started. Don't worry about the credit section, since you're paying cash." She slid a clipboard across the desk, and I sat in one of the cushy chairs and started filling out the forms. It was just some basic stuff, and they didn't even ask for my birthday. I guess they didn't care. There probably weren't too many underage kids trying to pay a grand to play with colored water.

Then I came to the blank that asked for my address. My pen stopped moving. I looked at Danitra, her head bent over some crazy tabloid, her extensions falling over her shoulders like red ropes. She was nice. I decided to risk it.

"Danitra?" I said in a low voice. "I just moved here, like, yesterday. I don't know what to put in the address part."

She looked up and frowned. "For real? Where you staying at?"

"The Strip," I said, hoping she wouldn't ask any more questions.

She shrugged. "So put the hotel address, if you want. But you don't want to be paying Strip prices. Why don't you get one of them monthly rentals? They got some on Harmon and Trop, go for like five hundred a month. My cousin Chanel stays there. You got to share a kitchen and bathroom, though, and sometimes they kinda nasty."

Five hundred a month! The number sank into my mind, practically glowing. For that, I could afford to eat, and get started on my job, and build up a better cushion. "What's the place called?" I asked.

Danitra flicked a page. "Harmon Terrace. They got all four-plexes along Harmon between Sandhill and Pecos. If one don't have a spot, you just drive down the road to the next one." She pointed at my clipboard. "You can leave the address blank and fill it in next time you come in."

"Thanks." I finished the form, handed it in, and paid her. Handing over the grand hurt, even for a good cause. I said, "Danitra? Is it hard to get a bartending job in this town?"

She gave a quiet snort. "Only for the ugly ones, baby. You ain't going to have any trouble at all. Not at all. Mmm-hmm." She shook her head and pursed her lips.

I gave her a huge smile.

"Go on now. You get yourself a place to live. See you next week." Danitra waved as I headed for the door. "You gonna do great here. Paul likes you already, I can tell."

I waved back and headed outside. The air felt amazing, and somehow the whole office park looked nicer, like somebody had been at it with a paint roller while I was inside. Paul already liked me. The other bartenders liked me. And I was going to prove them right.

Then a thought hit me, and I got a strange feeling. *Had I just found myself a new form of dealing?*

Well, the stuff in those pill bottles either got you hooked or did bad shit to your body, even in small amounts. Booze was different. It could hook people, all right, but plenty of people could handle their liquor, knew when to stop, just enjoyed a good drink.

Maybe this was what that bartender meant about handling your bar like a man. I didn't like to think about cutting people off, but maybe that was part of it. Maybe another part was pouring a lot of free coffee. Not letting people get in their cars wasted. Stepping in when guys tried to get stumbling-drunk girls to leave with them. Maybe it was other things, too. I guessed I'd find out.

CHAPTER TWENTY-TWO

By that night, I had moved into Four Horizons Apartments. It was money down, some papers to fill out, and no questions asked. I wasn't surprised; the place was so nasty, they should have paid people to live there instead of the other way around. It was a good thing my parking space was right under my window, because otherwise my car probably would have been ganked one part at a time, like food stolen by ants at a picnic.

Still, I felt like a king lying on my mattress, staring at the cottage cheese ceiling. There were three doors in the tiny room: one to the parking lot, which was full of hoopdies; one to the bathroom, which I shared with somebody who'd been using the same razor for about a century; and one to the kitchen, which had a sketchy, rotting smell and a refrigerator packed with Big Boy drumsticks.

But none of it mattered. I was on my own, not depending on Phil anymore, with plans that didn't involve sitting at a desk.

And I had Irina. Even though I knew it was stupid to hope, and we were seventeen, a long way from anything serious, I had this feeling I'd found my girl. I wished I'd introduced her to my mom when I had the chance.

Thinking of my mom made me throw a guilty look at my phone charging in the wall. She'd had time to settle down and was probably starting to worry. She might have even called some White Center people, trying to track me down. I picked up my cell and dialed home, bracing for a blowup.

Mom answered on the second ring. "Gabe, where are you? You can come home already. Phil's calmed down."

Like I was gone because I was worried about Phil. "I'm in Vegas." There was a crazy-long silence. "Mom?"

"*Las* Vegas? Nevada?"

"Yeah. I have to tell you some stuff."

As usual, she didn't listen right away. "Okay, I don't know what you're doing out there, I hope you had fun, but come home. I'm sorry we sprang the news on you like that. I've been thinking about it, and I should have told you alone, not with Phil sitting there."

"It wouldn't have made a difference."

"I know you don't like him, but honey, you didn't think he'd leave his wife, either. So maybe he's not as bad as you think."

I sighed. It was time for the bomb. "Mom, I dropped out of school. I'm staying in Vegas."

I could feel her shock waves all the way from Washington. "You . . . you . . . what?"

I guess there was a part of me that was still mad, because I said, "I can't live with Phil."

Mom took a shaky breath. "I'll leave him."

Immediately I felt horrible. "Mom, you don't have to—"

"No, you're my son. You can't drop out. I'll leave him."

I rolled onto my back and covered my eyes with my hand. "I'm sorry. I was being a jerk. It's not just Phil. I'm eighteen next month. I'd be leaving soon anyway. And I'm not cut out for school. I screwed up my finals."

"I'll talk to your tea—"

I cut her off. "I'd have to do summer school, and I'm not doing that. I'm going to get a good job in a restaurant, I'll make a ton of money. I'll get to talk to people all day . . . You know I can't do desk work." I heard a begging sound in my voice.

Mom said thickly, "I had this same conversation with your nana when I was sixteen. I guess I passed it down."

"You passed me down your big old cajones," I said, but she didn't laugh.

"What about tutoring? Your counselor said they have free tutoring. Or I can get Ph— I can pay for a tutor for you, a private one, not the ones at school." She'd almost said, *I can get Phil to pay for a tutor.*

If it hadn't been for his name slipped in, a tiny piece of me might have considered it. "No, I'm done for real. It isn't my scene."

"Gabe, you can't just quit. You're two quarters away from graduating." Mom's voice was shaking.

"Two quarters and summer school, and who knows if I'd pass my classes that time around, either! Mom, I'm done!" I took a breath and said slowly and clearly, "I am not. Coming home."

She started to cry.

My hand was twitching, I wanted to hang up so badly. "I'll do my GED," I said.

"It's not the same."

"That's what *you* did, right?"

"Yeah," she said, still crying. "Oh, Gabe."

"Mom, stop it!"

"I can't! I'm sad!"

"What's wrong with a GED?"

"It's just not the same. Hold on."

I groaned. "Not a quote."

But it was too late. I could hear the crinkle of pages. She read, "The rule seems to be that the bigger and more life-changing the decision, the less it will seem like a decision at all."

"I know I'm making a big decision! Is that what you're trying to say? I get it! I've been killing myself for years. I just can't keep going!"

The silence dragged on so long, it was even worse than her crying. Finally she said in a heavy voice, "You should sign up for the GED right away, while you still remember how to do the math and things."

"Okay," I agreed. I thought I might as well. I heard Mom blowing her nose on the other end.

"How do you plan to support yourself?" she asked.

"Bussing or waiting. And I'm going to bartending school . . . when I'm old enough."

"I always pictured you in a suit, with your own office. You're so smart, Gabe."

"You're my mom! You have to think that!" I said, almost shouting. "And what does smart have to do with it? Just because I'm smart, I can't be a bartender?"

"No, that's not—"

"No, seriously? How come everybody has this idea that the only way to 'succeed' is to choke in a tie and sit behind some desk all day, staring at a computer? Isn't it good enough just to do something I like?"

"It's about money," Mom said. "Money gives you the freedom to live how you want." I knew she was thinking of her own life, and how she had to hustle to get by.

"Well, bartenders make plenty of money. And they don't have to work eighty hours a week."

"Will bartending really make you happy?" She sounded as if she didn't think it would.

I started to answer, but she interrupted me. "Please, think about it before you say yes. Take Phil out of this. Just think about bartending. *Will it make you happy?*"

I tried to do what she said. I pictured myself boss of my own bar, talking with people all day, hanging out, making drinks, never sitting down. I *hated* sitting. Liked talking. Was good at being social. "Yes," I said.

"Then do a good job at it." Mom was crying again. And at that moment I decided I *would* do a good job. I'd be the best bartender ever.

She took a deep breath. "Where will you stay?"

"I got a place."

"*Already?* Where?"

"Some apartment."

"What's the neighborhood like?"

"Just regular." I thought it was best not to give too many details.

"What are you going to eat? You don't cook."

"Ding Dongs and Cheetos, Mom. C'mon, I can figure it out myself." I tried to sound annoyed, but I sort of liked that she was worried about my food.

After that, she wanted to know more details: what exactly my apartment looked like, whether it was clean, who were my neighbors. I may have stretched the truth a little, because I wasn't trying to give her a heart attack.

"What about Thanksgiving?" Mom got choked up again. "Are you coming home for Thanksgiving?"

I sighed. "No. I'll get a package of Oscar Mayer or something. You know I like sliced turkey better, anyway." Then we had to have a ten-minute conversation about what I should get for Thanksgiving that wouldn't require cooking.

When I hung up, I set down my phone and looked out the window into the parking lot. Part of me had always felt like I was born one down, having no dad and a featherhead mom. But the truth was, Mom came through when it mattered. She had said she would leave Phil. I knew the sound in her voice, and she was dead serious.

That was big. No, huge.

It's a good feeling to stop being pissed at your own mom.

I thought about the other people I should call: Missy, Kyle, Matt, Forrest. Missy would be jealous and ask when she could visit. Kyle and Forrest would think I was stupid for dropping out but cool for running off to Vegas. Matt would think I was stupid, period. I'd be one of those high school legends, who they all kind of laughed and shook their heads about. Or maybe they'd keep in touch. You never know. People can surprise you.

♠ ♣ ♥ ♦

My first mail from Irina came two days later. She'd called from a pay phone when she got home and asked for my address, said she wanted to send something. But I'd expected a letter, not a package.

It was in a padded yellow envelope, addressed in loopy writing. I slit it open with my keys. There were three things inside: a letter, a GED study guide, and a little wooden picture of an angel with a shiny gold halo. The angel was a guy, which was different, with light brown skin and dark hair, not like the blond ladies in white dresses you see at Christmas. His eyes were almond-shaped and dark brown, and he looked very serious. I stared at him and then opened Irina's letter.

Dear Gabe,

I miss you insanely. My mom said she'd get me a phone this week, so I should be able to call soon with my number. In the meantime, I don't want to talk on my parents' phone. I'm kind of paranoid. I'm sure you understand. Things have been so tense since I got back.

I told my parents I don't want to go to conservatory, and they're pretty upset right now. Like I'm not sure my dad is ever going to talk to me again. But I have to do this. I need four years on my own before I decide what I want to do with my life.

I don't think I want to be a professional musician. It's kind of scary to write that, because my whole life, everybody, including me, thought it was what I would end up doing. But

I keep feeling like it's the wrong path. Every time I imagine myself in conservatory, I feel blurry, fuzzy, and dull.

But when I think about going to college, everything gets clear, and I can actually imagine walking around campus, going to classes, and learning stuff. I see myself in a library inside a study carrel, for some reason.

Anyway, I've been researching colleges. I like Notre Dame, Dartmouth, and Penn, so far. I don't know if I'd like living in South Bend or Hanover, but Philadelphia sounds amazing . . . so maybe it's Penn if they'll have me.

How are you? I want to hear more about bartending school. It sounds hilarious. I was thinking about what you said about not wanting any job to own you, and wanting your off time to be really off. I think you and I want the same thing; we're just coming at it from different directions. We both want to dig deep into life, and not be on a mindless wheel, and actually enjoy our time here, and do something worthwhile, but not focus on money or being "big." I hope what you said about us comes true. You know what I'm talking about.

The GED book is the one that my parents bought for me when we were trying to decide if I should homeschool or just take the GED. It's really basic. I think you should just do it and get it over with.

The icon is of the Archangel Gabriel. I know you're not religious or anything, but Anya's mom gave me the icon when I got baptized, and it's special to me. Those Russian words on the back say, "Irinushka, Archangel Gabriel brought the news of salvation to mankind." Gabriel is your patron, and I just thought you should have at least one picture of him, even if

you don't believe in that stuff. I'm not out there, and it helps
to think he's watching over you. Also, I have kissed that icon
(bottom-left corner) at least a thousand times (icons are like
pictures of people we love), and so maybe in some way my kisses
are soaked into it.

Anyway, I miss you, I want to wrap my arms around you
and sleep in your arms . . . I want all kinds of things. I'll call
you later.
Love,
Irina

I stared at that word *love* for a long time before folding the letter
and putting it back in the envelope. A light, insanely happy feeling
boiled up in my chest. Irina wouldn't write anything by accident,
definitely not *love*. I checked my phone to make sure my ringer was
on, even though I knew it was. Then I took the angel picture and set
it on my window. I reached out and touched the bottom-left corner
and thought of Irina. She said he brought the news of salvation to
mankind. What did I need to be saved from? I thought about my
life and almost laughed. There were plenty of things—but mostly
from myself, I guessed.

LOOK FOR *OUT OF ACES,*

BOOK TWO IN THE BETTING BLIND SERIES,

IN 2015.

ABOUT THE AUTHOR

Stephanie Guerra is also the author of the young adult novel *Torn* and the middle-grade novel *Billy the Kid Is Not Crazy*. Stephanie teaches children's literature in the College of Education at Seattle University. She serves as the Seattle host for the teen fiction blog Readergirlz. In 2013, she was awarded the Virginia Hamilton Essay Award for her writing on multicultural literary experiences for youth. Her research focuses on literacy instruction for incarcerated and at-risk teens. Stephanie lives in Seattle, Washington, with her husband and children. Learn more: www.stephanieguerra.com.